HELLO, MALLORY

HELLO, MALLORY

Ann M. Martin

AN
APPLE
PAPERBACK

SCHOLASTIC INC.
New York Toronto London Auckland Sydney

Cover art by Hodges Soileau

No part of this publication may be reproduced in whole or in part, or stored in a retrieval system, or transmitted in any form or by any means, electronic, mechanical, photocopying, recording, or otherwise, without written permission of the publisher. For information regarding permission, write to Scholastic Inc., 555 Broadway, New York, NY 10012.

ISBN 0-590-25169-4

12 11 10 9 8 7 6 5 4 3 2   12   5 6 7 8 9/9 0/0

Printed in the U.S.A.   40

This book is
For M
From A
With Love

HELLO, MALLORY

CHAPTER 1

Spectacles. Eyeglasses. Bifocals. Trifocals. No matter what you call them, glasses are glasses, and I have to wear them.

Hello. I'm Mallory Pike. I'm eleven. Apart from the glasses, this is the thing you need to know about me: I have seven younger brothers and sisters. That's right, seven. And three of them are triplets, identical boys. If you think it's easy to blend in when you come from an eight-kid family, wear glasses, and furthermore are the only one you know with a head of curly hair, you're wrong.

The triplets are ten years old. Their names are Adam, Jordan, and Byron. Occasionally, they make me crazy, but mostly they're all right. The good thing about triplets is that they always have each other. Built-in friends.

The next kid in my family is Vanessa. Vanessa is nine and hopes to become a poet. Sometimes she goes around for days on end speaking in rhyme. Talk about making me crazy. But Vanessa is all right, too, and in a lot of ways we're very much alike.

My eight-year-old brother is Nicky. I feel kind of sorry for Nicky because he has trouble making a place for himself in our family. He wants to play with the triplets most of the time, since they're boys, but the triplets think Nicky is a baby. That leaves Nicky with us girls, and Nicky is going through this phase where he *hates* girls.

Margo is seven. *She's* going through a bossy phase, even though she's almost the youngest in the family. She bosses everyone and everything, even my parents, her dolls, and Pow, this dog that lives down the street. It's always "Do this," and "Do that." Mostly, we ignore her. I mean we ignore the bossiness, not Margo herself.

Last in our family is Claire. Claire is five. I guess being the baby in a big family isn't always easy, but you'd think she wouldn't exactly need to draw attention to herself. That's just what Claire does, though, by being extremely silly. Over the summer, she started calling our parents Moozie and Daggles instead of Mommy and Daddy, and she attaches "silly-billy-goo-goo" to people's names. Like, if she wants a drink, she'll say, "Can I have some juice, Mallory-silly-billy-goo-goo?" Sometimes she'll add, "Puh-lease, puh-lease, with a cherry on top?" It's annoying, but at least she doesn't do it as often as she used to. Besides, Claire is huggable and affectionate, so it's easy to overlook the "silly-billy-goo-goo" stuff.

Then there are my parents. My mom doesn't have a job. I mean, a job outside of the house, like being a doctor or an insurance salesperson or something. She says us kids are her job, and that with eight of us it's a big job.

My dad is a lawyer, but not the kind you see on TV, making wild speeches in a crowded courtroom. He's what's called a corporate lawyer. He's the lawyer for a big company in Stamford, Connecticut. (We live in Stoneybrook, Connecticut, which isn't far away.) Mostly, he sits at a desk or attends meetings. Once in awhile, though, he does go to court, but I bet he doesn't make speeches. I think he just stands up a lot and says, "Objection!" and things like that.

Every single one of us Pikes, even my parents, has dark brown hair (Mom calls it "chestnut brown" to make it seem less ordinary) and blue eyes. Nicky and Vanessa and I wear glasses (all the time — not just for reading, unfortunately), but as I mentioned earlier, I am the only one with curly hair. I'm also the only one with freckles across my nose. I really stick out. If only Mom would let me get contacts. But she won't. Not until I'm fifteen. And she won't let me get my ears pierced until I'm thirteen.

Being eleven is a real trial.

I will admit one thing, though: No matter what age you are, being the oldest of eight kids sure teaches you responsibility. And it taught me a lot about baby-sitting. I love sitting, even though I haven't done much of it on my own yet. But guess what? These girls I know asked me if I'd be interested in joining their baby-sitting club! And they're not just any girls, they're *older* girls! No kidding. There are four of them and they live in my neighborhood. (Well, most of them do.) Their names are Kristy Thomas, Claudia Kishi, Mary Anne Spier, and Dawn Schafer. They used to have a fifth member, Stacey McGill, but she moved away. That's why the girls need me — to take Stacey's place. The way they know me is that they sit for our family all the time. Although lately, instead of being sat for, I've helped with the sitting. And as I said, I know a lot about kids.

I am *so flattered* that the girls want me to join their club. But I'm nervous, too. What if they decide I'm not good enough or not grown-up enough or something? Oh, well. I'll know on

Monday. That's when I go to my first club meeting.

Right now it's Saturday. Two days to wait. But I've got plenty to do. I'm reading three books — *Dr. Dolittle*, *The Incredible Journey*, and this really funny one called *Freaky Friday*. I love to read, and I don't believe that you have to finish one book before you start another. I like to write, too. I keep journals, and I write stories, stories, stories. Sometimes I illustrate them.

Plus, this afternoon, I have to baby-sit. In fact, I better go downstairs now. Dad is taking the triplets to the barber for haircuts, and Mom is taking Margo and Vanessa shopping for sneakers. That leaves me in charge of Nicky and Claire. I guess I'm lucky that my parents pay me for taking care of my own brothers and sisters.

It was time to hide my journal (not easy, since I share a room with Vanessa). I put the book in its usual spot under my mattress. (I bet Vanessa knows where I keep it.) Then I ran down the stairs.

"Oh, there you are, honey," said Mom. "Good. Your father and I are just about to leave. Nicky's in the backyard with Buddy Barrett. You know where we'll be, right?"

"At Mr. Gates' and at Bellair's," I replied.

(Mr. Gates is the barber; Bellair's is a department store.)

"Right," said Mom.

"Moozie-silly-billy-goo-goo, I want shoes, too," whined an unhappy voice. It was Claire. She was slogging up the stairs from the rec room, looking dismal.

My mother turned around and took Claire's chin in her hand. "You don't need sneakers, sweetie," she said. "When you've outgrown your red ones, then you can have a new pair."

"Not fair," grumbled Claire, heading back down the stairs. "Silly-billy-goo-goo."

"Don't worry, Mom," I said. "I can handle her."

And I could. Dad drove off with the triplets, Mom drove off with my sisters, and I took Claire into the backyard with a bottle of soap bubbles. Claire blew bubbles and forgot about shoes, and Nicky played volleyball with his friend Buddy (Buddy is Pow the dog's owner) and forgot about us girls, which seemed to be a perfect arrangement for everyone.

"Foo, foo," went Claire, making bubbles stream from the plastic wand. "Look, Mallory-silly-billy-goo-goo!"

Slam, slam went the volleyball as the boys pounded it back and forth over the net. They

6

weren't fooling around. Their game was serious.

The boys were still playing when my father came back with the triplets. The car pulled to a stop in the driveway. The doors opened slowly. Claire and I looked on with interest. My brothers hate getting their hair cut.

"You look like a nerd," said Adam, punching Jordan on the arm and laughing riotously.

"Me! You're looking in a mirror," retorted Jordan. "You look just the same . . . only worse."

The boys tried to sneak into the house without being noticed, but Buddy caught sight of them and let out a howl of laughter. "Ha-ha! Ha-ha!" The volleyball game didn't stop, though.

"Pay attention, Buddy!" Nicky yelled. He slammed the ball over the net.

Since Buddy was laughing at the triplets, he wasn't really ready. But he managed to return the ball. "Oof!" he groaned. "There you are, you show-off. I hit it anyw—"

"Ow! Ow, ow, ow!" Now Nicky wasn't ready. He hadn't expected Buddy to return his shot, and he'd caught sight of the triplets with their haircuts. The ball had sailed over the net fast and hard. It whammed into Nicky's outstretched hand, and smashed his fingers.

"*Ow!*" he cried again. "My hand!"

Nicky sounded terrified. Dad, my brothers, Claire, and I all ran to him.

"Ow! Ow!" Nicky continued to shriek. He doubled over, clutching his hand to his stomach.

"Let me see, Nick-o," said my father, easing Nicky's hand toward him.

We all stared. Nicky's pointer finger was sticking out from his hand at a strange angle.

"Oh, no," I said with a gasp.

"Broken," said Dad briskly.

Buddy burst into tears. "I'm sorry, Nicky. I'm sorry," he kept saying.

Mom drove up just then. She saw the crowd in our yard, rushed over to us (along with Margo and Vanessa), took one look at Nicky's finger, and said, "Emergency room. Mallory, you're in charge."

My brothers and sisters and I just stood in the yard with our mouths open while Mom and Dad carried Nicky to the station wagon and backed down the driveway. The only one making any noise was Buddy, who was still crying.

I remembered Mom's words, "Mallory, you're in charge," and decided I'd better act like it. First, I calmed down Buddy and sent him

8

home. Then I told the others to go inside and that I would fix them a snack.

When things were under control, I sank into a chair in the living room for a few minutes.

Wouldn't the girls in the Baby-sitters Club be proud of me? I thought. I was taking care of six of my brothers and sisters all by myself. None of the other girls had ever done that, since Mom insists on two sitters if more than five kids need to be taken care of.

Two hours later, Nicky returned.

"Look!" he said, marching proudly into the kitchen, Mom and Dad at his heels.

"What's that?" asked Claire, peering at his hand.

"A cast. My finger was broken in two places. They took X rays."

"He was very brave," said Mom.

Nicky's cast was a complicated thing covering most of his finger and hand, and positioning the finger in a way that looked pretty uncomfortable. But Nicky didn't mind. He was waiting for Monday so he could show off his injury in school.

And I was waiting for Monday so I could brag to the girls in the Baby-sitters Club about my unexpected job.

CHAPTER 2

Monday morning at last! Sunday had seemed like the longest day of my life. I had finished *Freaky Friday*, read three more chapters of *The Incredible Journey*, and written a story about a frog in a rainstorm called "Rainy Days and Froggy Nights." I had entertained Nicky and baked cookies with Margo. When all that was done it was still only four o'clock in the afternoon.

But now Monday had arrived. I leaped out of bed and flung open my closet door. I wondered what a person was supposed to wear to a baby-sitting meeting with thirteen-year-olds. I decided I should look just a little dressed up. I thought about Claudia and the other girls in the club. I was pretty sure that when they got dressed up, they wore trendy clothes like big, bright sweater-dresses or sparkly tops and tight pants. I don't have any clothes like that. Mom says I'm too young. Maybe when I'm twelve or thirteen.

Well, I could look nice anyway. After standing in front of the closet for so long that Vanessa made a pig face at me while *she* chose *her* clothes, I finally decided on my red jumper that said *Mallory* across the front, a short-sleeved white blouse, and white tights with little red hearts all over them.

"You look like a Valentine," Vanessa told me, but I didn't care.

I put on my penny loafers.

"Mallory!" said Mom, as I sat down at the breakfast table a little while later. "You look lovely. . . . This isn't school-picture day, is it?" she added, glancing suspiciously at my brothers and sisters. They certainly were not dressed in their best clothes.

"No, Mom. Don't worry," I told her. "I'm going to the Baby-sitters Club meeting, remember?"

"Oh, that's right. Well, have fun."

Have fun, I thought. Sure. I was as jumpy as a cat.

When I got to Stoneybrook Middle School that morning I looked around for Kristy, Dawn, Mary Anne, and Claudia. I thought that if I saw them, I could just walk up to them, as cool as anything, and say, "Hi, you guys. How is everything? Can't wait for the meeting." I could pretend I was a big eighth-grader instead of a twerpy sixth-grader.

But the sixth-grade wing is at the opposite end of the building from the eighth-grade wing. There was no chance I'd see them unless I took a little walk. I pretended I needed to go to the library, which is near the eighth-grade wing. As I wandered through the halls, I looked and looked for the girls, but I didn't see them. Not in the library, not outside the cafeteria, not hanging around the gym. I was still only halfway back to my homeroom when the bell rang.

The bell! I'd been fooling around longer than I thought. I tore through the halls to my classroom and darted through the door just before Mrs. Frederickson closed it. I was the last to arrive and slid into my seat between bossy Benny Ott and Rachel Robinson. (Mrs. Frederickson seats us alphabetically.)

Wait a second. I wasn't between Benny and Rachel. I was between Benny and some girl I'd never seen before. Rachel was one seat away from me. What was wrong? I checked my desk. Yup. It was the one I always sit at, with the big E.L. carved in an upper corner and the heart carved in a lower one.

I took another look at the girl sitting next to me. My eyes widened. For one thing, the girl was beautiful. She was long-legged and thin, and even sitting down she appeared graceful.

Also, she was black.

There were no black students in our entire grade. This new girl would be the only one. In fact, there are only about six black kids in the whole school. They're in the seventh and eighth grades.

Wow. This was pretty interesting.

"Class," Mrs. Frederickson said, rapping on her desk with a pencil. "Good morning. As you've probably noticed, we have a new student. Her name is Jessica Ramsey. Our seating has changed a bit to make room for her. Jessica is sitting at Rachel Robinson's old desk, and Rachel and everyone after her have moved over one seat."

I saw Rachel cross her eyes at Jessica, tilt her head to the side, and stick her tongue out. If Jessica noticed, she didn't pay attention. She just kept looking straight ahead at Mrs. Frederickson.

Why, I wondered, did Rachel care about her desk so much? We only sit at these desks during homeroom. We don't even keep stuff in them, since other classes use them the rest of the day.

"I hope," Mrs. Frederickson went on, "that you will make Jessica feel welcome." Mrs. Frederickson sounded sincere, but I noticed that she didn't ask Jessica to stand up and introduce herself and tell us where she had come from. That was what she had done when Benny Ott was new. From day one, we'd known that Benny was from Detroit, and that his dad sold car parts and his mom was a secretary and Benny hoped to become a great actor.

Jessica Ramsey sat next to me, a mystery. I kept looking at her long legs. Maybe she was a dancer or a gymnast or something. Of course, I looked at her face, too. Jessica's eyes were huge and dark. Her lashes were so long I wondered if they were fake. Probably not, if her mother was anything like mine, and I decided that was a distinct possibility, since Jessica wore glasses and didn't have pierced ears, either.

I wondered what being the only black student in your grade would feel like. I guessed it would feel no different from being the only anything in your grade. I was the only one in our grade with seven brothers and sisters, including ten-year-old triplets. But I knew that wasn't quite the same. The kids couldn't tell that just by looking at me. But Jessica's coffee-colored skin was there for the world to see.

However, I didn't think nearly as much about Jessica's skin as I did about the fact that a new girl was finally in our class. I'd been waiting for this.

I needed a best friend.

I'm pretty friendly with most of the kids in our grade, but I don't have a best friend. For one thing, all the other girls already have best friends. There aren't any loose ones floating around. For another, I spend so much time with my brothers and sisters, and reading and writing, that I'd never needed a best friend. Lately, though, I'd decided it would be nice. However, my only shot was with a new kid, and the only new kid in our class had been yucky Benny Ott — until Jessica arrived.

Jessica caught me looking at her and gave me a shy smile. I smiled back, just as shyly. Was this the way things started between best friends? It wasn't a bad start; it just seemed like such a small step. . . .

The bell rang, and with clatters and crashes, my classmates tore out of the room. Benny went so fast he knocked his chair over and had to run back and stand it up again. By the time he had righted his chair, Jessica was gone. I'd been so busy watching Benny that I'd

15

missed seeing Jessica leave. And I was disappointed. I'd been hoping I could help her find her next class. Someone else must have helped her.

My first class of the day was social studies and Jessica wasn't in it. Second period was English, and as I took my seat in the back of the room, I saw Jessica slip into a seat in the third row. I also saw Benny Ott shoot four rubber bands at the back of her head that period. Jessica made no sign of feeling them. And Mr. Williams, the teacher, pretended he didn't see, either.

Third period, gym — no Jessica.

Fourth period, math — no Jessica.

Fifth period was lunch. Since the hot lunch costs under a dollar, my parents make me and my brothers and sisters buy it every day (or else make our own). Mom says she has better things to do than pack eight lunches five mornings a week.

It was spaghetti day. I paid for my meal and carried my tray to a long table where a bunch of girls from my homeroom were sitting. Almost all of them looked up and said, "Hello, Mallory." That was nice, but what I was longing for was someone who would leap out of her chair squealing, "Oh! Oh, Mal! You'll never in a million years guess what happened!"

16

In other words, a best friend.

I sat down next to Rachel Robinson. Rachel and three others turned away and put their heads together, whispering. I was curious, but I was also starving. I opened my carton of milk.

"Mallory," whispered Rachel.

"What?" I stuffed half a meatball in my mouth.

"Can you believe that new girl?" Rachel sounded aghast.

"Who, Jessica Ramsey?" I replied.

"What do you mean 'who'? Of course I mean Jessica Ramsey. Who else?"

I shrugged. "What about her?"

"What *about* her?" cried Sally, this girl I've never really liked. "Are you blind? She's *black*."

I nearly choked. "So?"

"Well, she doesn't, you know, belong here."

"Where?" I challenged them. "She doesn't belong where?"

Sally shrugged uncomfortably. "Oh, I don't know. . . ."

"What are you so upset for, anyway?" Rachel asked me.

I tried to compose myself. I ate some spaghetti. "I am not upset," I said at last.

I wanted to change the subject, but before I could, Anita (Rachel's best friend) said, giggling around a mouthful of bread, "Where do you think Jessica moved from — Africa?"

For some reason, the other girls thought this was hysterical.

"I bet her real name is Mobobwee or something," added Sally.

I wanted to get up and move, but I didn't. Anyway, the girls lost interest in Jessica. They started talking about TV shows and rock stars.

I didn't listen. I watched Jessica instead. She ate by herself, reading a book at the same time. I wondered what she was reading.

The day wore on.

Sixth period, French — no Jessica.

Seventh period, study hall — no Jessica.

Eight period, science. Jessica was in the class! There was even more hope for a best friend. But by then I was too excited to think about Jessica. School was nearly over. It was almost time for my first meeting of the Baby-sitters Club!

CHAPTER 3

Today was our first meeting with Mallory instead of Stacey. It was a little weird. Sorry, Mallory, but it was. Stacey was in the club from the beginning. She was at our first official meeting, and she hardly missed a single meeting after that. She even came to the one we held the day before she moved back to New York City, when she couldn't take sitting jobs anymore. That's real dedication.

Mallory, I'm not sure how to say this, but you don't have to get dressed up for our meetings, I mean if you don't want to. The rest of us don't. We just wear our school clothes. Sometimes we change out of our school clothes into even more casual things. And, really there's no reason to be nervous. You know all of us. We've baby-sat together before, and Mary Anne's even gone on vacation with your family. So relax!

Wow. I didn't realize Kristy could see how nervous I was. I had no idea I'd be overdressed, either. You should have seen what the other girls had on. I'll describe the kind of clothes they wear when I introduce them to you. But first I better explain about that diary Kristy was writing in. It's the Baby-sitters Club notebook, and it's very important.

The girls really run the club professionally. When I think of clubs, I think of fooling around in the kitchen making fudge and giggling and gossiping and maybe collecting dues so you have enough money for a slumber party or something. The girls in the Baby-sitters Club do some stuff like that — and more. Baby-sitting is a *business* for them. The dues they collect are for expenses, such as paying Kristy's big brother Charlie to drive her to and from meetings, since she moved across town last summer. And they have lots of clients who call on them when they need sitters, *and* the club members earn pretty much money.

Anyway, back to the notebook. Kristy says every sitter has to write up each job she goes on. They write about what happened, any problems, and stuff the rest of us might need to know, like if one of the kids has an allergy or is afraid of the dark or spiders or loud noises. Then the notebook — which is very fat — is passed around so the others can read about all the sitting jobs. Sometimes they write about important club meetings, too.

The girls also keep a record book where they write down information about their clients, keep track of the money they earn, and, of course, schedule their sitting appointments.

Kristy Thomas is the president of the club, since the club was her idea. She seemed to be the most casually dressed of all the girls at the meeting. She was wearing faded jeans, sneakers, a pale pink turtleneck, and a dark pink sweater. I've seen her wear clothes like that an awful lot. Kristy is really nice. Whenever she used to baby-sit for me, I could count on fun. But sometimes she's a little bossy. Not bossy in a baby way like my sister Margo, but bossy in an adult way. Twice during the meeting she interrupted what was going on so she could straighten problems out. She didn't listen to what anyone else had to say. She just jumped in — boom — and said, "No more discussion. This is what we're going to do." Wow. Just so you know, Kristy has brown hair and brown eyes. And I guess her mother doesn't let her wear makeup because her face is always plain. Apart from her mom, she has a (rich) step-father, a younger brother named David Michael, two big brothers, Sam and Charlie, and a little stepsister and stepbrother, Karen and Andrew. Also a dog, Shannon, and a cat, Boo-Boo. They live in her stepfather's big house, which Kristy says is a mansion.

The vice-president of the club is Claudia Kishi. Claudia is really something. She's absolutely gorgeous. I'd give anything to be as pretty as she is. Her parents are originally from Japan and she has these black, black eyes, silky black, black hair, and a complexion as perfectly smooth as cream. I guess her parents aren't as strict as Kristy's mother and stepfather because Claudia has pierced ears, uses makeup, and wears clothes my mother wouldn't even let me look at in stores, much less buy. Things like short, tight pants with little ballet slippers, or torn T-shirts decorated with sequins, or overalls and high-topped sneakers. And her jewelry! She has a bracelet that looks like a coiled snake, and earrings that are a dog for one ear and a bone for the other, and I don't know what else. Claudia is a fun baby-sitter, too, because she loves art. Sometimes when Claudia would come over, she'd help my brothers and sisters and me make murals or holiday decorations or even papier-mâché. I don't know too much else about Claudia except that she likes to read mysteries, and someone once said she's not a very good student. Which is unfortunate, since her big sister Janine is a genius. Claudia and Janine live with their parents and their grandmother, Mimi. The club meetings are always held in Claudia's room because she has a private phone and a private phone number. (Lucky duck.) I think that's also why she's the vice-president.

Mary Anne Spier is the club secretary. Mary Anne is petite and neat and precise. Her job is to keep the record book in order, and she's good at it. Mary Anne may not be the most fun of all the baby-sitters, but I think she's the nicest. She's sensitive. (Maybe she's shy, too. I'm not sure.) And she's patient. You know you could go to Mary Anne if you had a problem or needed help with your homework. One funny thing is that she's almost the exact opposite of Kristy — yet they're best friends. Kristy is loud and sometimes bossy, Mary Anne is quiet and never, ever bossy. Kristy likes to be the center of attention, Mary Anne once ran away from her own surprise birthday party. However, Mary Anne does look a little like Kristy, with her wavy brown hair and brown eyes, but she dresses better. She's not really trendy, but at least she puts on something besides the same jeans all the time. On the day of my first meeting, she was wearing a baggy yellow sweater with a silver squiggle pin near the collar, a short skirt made out of sweat-shirt material, yellow tights, and ballet slippers. Not outrageous, though, and I know exactly why. Mary Anne lives with her dad and her kitten, Tigger. Her mom died a long, long time ago, and I think Mr. Spier is strict with Mary Anne sometimes. He even used to make her wear her hair in braids, but he's much better about things like that now.

The last club member is Dawn Schafer. She's also the newest. She and her mom and her younger brother Jeff moved to Connecticut less than a year ago. They moved because Dawn's parents got divorced. And they moved all the way from California! Poor Dawn. I'd hate it if *I* had to move *to* California, but Dawn seems pretty happy here. Her brother Jeff is a different story. I know because he's a friend of the triplets. They say he's been in lots of trouble in school lately, and that all he wants is to move back to his dad. That must be hard on Dawn — to think that her brother would rather live with her father than with her and Mrs. Schafer. Anyway, Dawn is the treasurer of the club. Stacey used to be treasurer, but when she moved away, Dawn took over for her. (I'm not sure what Dawn's job used to be. Nothing too important, I guess. Maybe she was just another sitter.) Dawn has long, pale, pale, pale blonde hair. I've never seen such long hair. It goes way down her back. She wears kind of casual clothes, like baggy jeans with the cuffs rolled up, shirts with the tails out, and big belts. And get this — she lives in a house that might be *haunted* and has a *secret passage!*

That's everybody in the club. Four thirteen-year-old, eighth-grade girls. They were sprawled around Claudia's room by the time I — the lowly eleven-year-old, sixth-grade girl — arrived.

"Hi," I said nervously, giving a little wave.

"Hi, Mallory," Dawn replied warmly. (I know Dawn pretty well since she lives right near me.)

"Hi," said Kristy, Claudia, and Mary Anne.

They sounded friendly. Even so, I felt completely out of place.

"Have a seat," said Kristy.

I looked around to see where the other girls were sitting. Kristy, who was wearing this visor and had stuck a pencil over one ear, was perched on a director's chair. Dawn and Mary Anne were lounging on Claudia's bed, and Claudia was kneeling on the floor, frowning, pawing through a pillowcase. Suddenly her frown turned to a smile and she yanked a handful of Tootsie Pops out of the pillowcase, then shoved it under her bed.

"Here they are!" she exclaimed.

She handed one to me as I sat gingerly on the floor. It was hard to find a comfortable position in my short jumper.

"Thanks," I said.

Claudia passed around the candy. Everyone took a lollipop except for Dawn, who tries to stick to health food.

"This is the first thing you should know about the club," Kristy said to me with a grin. "Our vice-president is a junk-food addict. She has stuff hidden all over her room. Lucky for us, she never minds sharing."

All I could do was smile. I couldn't think of a thing to say.

Kristy's grin faded. She rubbed her hands together in a businesslike way. "Well," she said, and I noticed that the others sat up a little straighter and paid attention. "We wanted you to come to the meeting today, Mallory, for two reasons. First, so you can see what our club is like and how it runs, and second, so we can decide, if, um, if . . ."

I knew she meant if I was good enough to be a part of the club, but I couldn't say so, and

I guess she couldn't, either. Not tactfully, anyway.

"What she means," Dawn spoke up, "is so we can get an idea of how much, um, how much . . ."

"How much experience you've had," Mary Anne finally filled in. She looked pleased with herself.

"Right," agreed Kristy, brightening. "And to find out how you handle certain situations. That kind of thing."

I nodded. "Well, I've been taking care of my brothers and sisters for years. I know how to change diapers and I know how to fix formulas. I've always —"

Ring, ring.

"I'll get it!" cried Kristy, Dawn, Mary Anne, and Claudia, all lunging for the phone.

Claudia reached it first.

I watched with interest. This was probably what a club meeting was *really* about.

"Good afternoon. Baby-sitters Club," said Claudia, sounding quite grown-up. "Mm-hmm. Mm-hmm. . . . Tuesday? I'll get right back to you. . . . Okay. 'Bye." Claudia hung up and turned to the rest of us. "Mrs. Perkins needs a sitter for Myriah and Gabbie next Tuesday from three-thirty to five-thirty."

Mary Anne was thumbing through the record book. She opened to the appointment calendar. "Claudia, you're the only one free. Want the job?"

"Sure!" she said.

"Oh," Kristy broke in. "Mallory, why don't you go with her? It can be a trial job for you, so one of us can see how you do."

"Okay!" I replied happily.

Claudia called Mrs. Perkins back to tell her who'd be sitting.

"And that's pretty much what we do at the meetings," Kristy said to me. "Just take job calls like that one and assign sitters. Oh, and collect dues and discuss problems."

I nodded again. Suddenly I remembered something. "Oh! I almost forgot to tell you," I said, feeling proud. "On Saturday, I baby-sat for *six* of my brothers and sisters by my*self*."

"You *did?*" said Dawn, looking impressed.

"How come?" asked Kristy.

I explained about Nicky's accident.

Kristy's eyes narrowed. So did her lips as she set them in a straight line. "Mallory," she said coolly. "That accident shouldn't have happened. You were in charge of Nicky. You should have been watching him."

"But I —"

"We can't have accidents happening when we're on the job," Kristy went on. She looked at the other girls and they nodded in agreement.

"Mallory," Dawn said gently, "we have to be really careful about who we accept in the club. We've had some trouble in the past — with sitters who weren't too reliable."

"But I *am* reliable," I said. "And I *was* watching Nicky. And I know *every*thing about taking care of kids." I probably shouldn't have said that last sentence, but I was desperate. There was this sinking feeling in my stomach.

"Well, there's one way to find out about that," said Kristy, frowning thoughtfully. "We'll give you a test. Can you come back tomorrow to take it?"

"S-sure," I stammered. A *test*? I had to take a *test*? "What kind of test?" I asked.

"It'll be a . . . surprise," said Kristy, and I knew she didn't have any baby-sitting test ready. She was going to have to make one up.

I must have looked awful, because Mary Anne changed the subject then. "Guess what," she said brightly. "A family moved into Stacey's old house."

"Really?" asked Claudia with interest.

Mary Anne nodded. "I passed by when the moving van was unloading."

"I can't imagine anybody but Stacey living in that house," said Claudia.

"I can't, either," said Mary Anne. "I didn't see them, only the moving men, but my dad told me it's a black family."

A black family! Maybe it was Jessica Ramsey's. That would be interesting. But I was too nervous to feel excited about it. All I could think of was the test. A baby-sitting test. Would I pass it? Or would I blow my chances with the club forever?

CHAPTER 4

The only good thing about taking the Baby-sitters Club test the next afternoon was that I didn't have to worry about what to wear to it. I threw on a pair of jeans, a sweat shirt that said I'D RATHER BE WRITING MY NOVEL, and a pair of sneakers. I figured I wouldn't look any better or worse than Kristy, and she was the president.

All day I was nervous, nervous, nervous. What kind of test would they give me? A real-life test like when you have to jump into a swimming pool and pull someone to the side? A written test? Or would they just sit there and ask me questions? I might do well on a written test, but I wasn't sure about the other kinds. I thought I'd be awfully scared. And who was going to give me the test? Kristy had said to go to club headquarters, which was Claudia's room. Would just Kristy and Claudia be there? Would everybody be there? Ooh, I am such a worrywart.

I felt like a baby.

I was so keyed up that I left my house forty-five minutes before test-time, and it only takes ten minutes to walk to the Kishis'. Halfway there, I realized what I could do with the extra thirty-five minutes. I could walk by Stacey McGill's old house and look for the new family.

So I did.

And guess what. Sitting right on Stacey's front stoop was Jessica Ramsey with a younger girl and a baby boy!

Jessica saw me at the same time I saw her. We smiled. Then we waved. I hesitated. At last I walked across the lawn to the stoop.

"Hi," I said. "I'm Mallory Pike. . . . You probably know that. I mean, but I wasn't sure. You must have met an awful lot of kids yesterday and today."

"I have. But I remember your name."

"I remember yours, too. Jessica. Jessica Ramsey."

"Right." Jessica grinned. "Call me Jessi, though."

"Okay. Hi, Jessi."

We laughed.

"I'm Becca," spoke up the other girl. Becca

looked like she was eight or nine years old. She was a younger version of Jessi, with those long legs and long eyelashes. "My real name is Rebecca, though," she told me. "See? Mama took the 'ca' off the end of Jessica's name and the 'Re' off the beginning of my name, and that's where our nicknames came from."

"Oh," I said. "I like that. I don't have a nickname. Not a real one, anyway. But sometimes people call me 'Mal.' " I looked at the little boy in Jessi's lap. He was chewing on a red plastic ring. "Who's that?" I asked.

Jessi turned the baby around so he was facing me. "This," she said fondly, "is Squirt. He's our brother."

"Squirt!" I couldn't help exclaiming.

"Well, his real name is John Philip Ramsey, Junior, but that seemed much too long for a kid. Besides, he was only five pounds, eight ounces when he was born."

"Oh," I said, understanding. "I get it. A little squirt."

"Right," agreed Becca. "You're smart."

"How old is Squirt?" I asked.

Squirt looked up at me with gigantic brown eyes and drooled down his shirt.

"Fourteen months," Becca replied, even though I'd asked Jessi.

Jessi wiped Squirt's chin.

"And I'm eight and a half," Becca went on. "How old are you?"

"Eleven," I said. "Same as your sister." I checked my watch. Plenty of time before I had to take that dumb baby-sitting test.

Jessi moved over and I sat next to her and Squirt on the stoop, while Becca found a hula hoop and began whirling it around her waist and knees.

"When did you move in?" I asked Jessi.

"Saturday," she replied. "Three days ago. Feels like three years. The house is a huge mess." She paused. "Do you like jokes?"

"Sure," I replied.

"Okay. Listen to this one. A farmer is driving down a highway and he sees a truck by the side of the road. It's got a flat tire, and the driver, who is holding a penguin, looks really upset, so the farmer pulls up and says 'Can I help you?' And the driver says, 'Oh, yes, please. I'm taking this penguin to the zoo. It's right down the road. Could you take him there for me while I wait for the tow truck?' The farmer says, 'Sure,' takes the penguin, and drives off. The next day the driver is going down a street and he sees the farmer with the penguin. 'What are you doing?' he cries. 'You were supposed to take that penguin to the

34

zoo!' The farmer smiles. 'I did,' he answers, 'and he had so much fun that today I'm taking him to the circus!' "

I burst out laughing and so did Squirt.

"He didn't understand that, did he?" I asked, amazed.

"Nah," replied Jessi. "He just laughs when other people do. By the way, I think he likes you."

Squirt was reaching out to me with chubby hands.

"Can I hold him?" I asked.

" 'Course." Jessi plopped Squirt in my lap, and he smiled and proudly blew spit bubbles. When he started to get wiggly, I set him on the lawn and Becca held his hands while he walked unsteadily around the yard.

"He's so close," said Jessi, watching her brother. "He'll be walking alone any day now."

Jessi's smile faded and she sat thoughtfully for awhile.

"So," I said. "Where'd you move from?"

"New Jersey. Oakley, New Jersey. My dad was offered a really great job here in Connecticut. That's how come we moved. I wish we were still in Oakley, though."

I nodded. "It must be hard to have to make new friends."

"Plus, we left all our relatives behind."

35

"Oh, wow."

"Yeah. Right on our street lived my grandma and grandpa, three aunts, two uncles, and my cousins Kara, Keisha, Sandy, Molly, Raun, Bill, and Isaac. Keisha was my cousin *and* my best friend. We even have the same birthday. June thirtieth. Hey, do you know how many stupids it takes to change a lightbulb?"

"No. How many?"

"Three. One to hold the lightbulb and two to turn his legs."

I burst out laughing again, and Squirt and Becca joined me.

"That is my most favorite joke," Becca informed me. "Jessi knows more jokes than anyone in the world."

"Well, not *that* many," said Jessi modestly.

"Do you want to be a comedienne or something when you grow up?" I asked.

"Oh, no *way!*" cried Jessi. "I'm going to be a ballet dancer."

I *knew* it. Those long legs of hers were a dead giveaway.

"I just went on toe," Jessi added proudly. "I've been dancing since I was four. You want to see my toe shoes?"

"Sure," I replied. I hesitated. "What are toe shoes?"

Jessi stood up. "Come on inside. I'll show

you. You can meet my mother, too. She'll be really happy to see you."

"She will?"

"Well, yeah. The neighbors haven't exactly dropped by to introduce themselves. We haven't met anybody around here yet."

"Oh. . . ." I wasn't sure what to say to that.

"Be warned," added Jessi as she opened the front door. "The house really *is* a mess. It looks like the movers threw everything in the windows and then left in a hurry."

I giggled. I like people who can make me laugh.

"Mama?" Jessi called.

I followed her inside. I'd only been in Stacey's house a few times. Still, it was weird to see someone else's furniture in it. And Jessi wasn't kidding. The place did look like the movers had thrown everything in the windows and left in a hurry.

"I'm in the dining room," a voice answered Jessi.

Jessi led me through the messy living room and into the messy dining room.

"Mama," she said, "this is Mallory Pike. She's in some of my classes at school."

I stepped forward and held out my hand the way Mom and Dad have taught us to do when we meet new people.

For just a second, Mrs. Ramsey looked surprised. Then her face relaxed into a smile. "Nice to meet you, Mallory," she said.

"Call her Mal, Mama," Jessi said, glancing at me. "That's her nickname."

"Do you live nearby, Mal?" asked Mrs. Ramsey.

We don't exactly. I tried to explain where our street is.

"We're going upstairs, Mama," Jessi said a few minutes later. "I want to show Mal my toe shoes and my room."

"Good luck finding either one," called Mrs. Ramsey as Jessi and I ran upstairs.

Jessi's room was actually in pretty good shape. At least, her furniture was in place and her posters were on her walls. And while it didn't look as if she'd unpacked her suitcases yet, I noticed that the books on her shelf were neatly organized.

"Wow," I said, gazing around. "Besides ballet, I guess you like horses and horse stories."

"Any stories, actually."

"Oh, me, too!" I said. "I love to read. You know, we have a lot in common. I mean, the reading and the horses. I don't take ballet lessons, though."

"We both wear glasses," Jessi pointed out.

"Yeah, but you're not wearing them now."

"I only need them for reading."

"My mom won't let me get pierced ears," I said. "Will yours?"

"Nope. But — get this — I have to have braces."

I couldn't believe it. "Me, too!" I cried again. "Next year. And we're both the oldest in our families. Hey, do you like kids?"

"Definitely," replied Jessi. "I was just starting to baby-sit for my little cousins when we left Oakley."

"Too bad."

I was about to tell Jessi about the Baby-sitters Club and my test when she said, "What's your favorite horse story?"

"*A Morgan for Melinda*," I answered without even needing to think about it.

"Oh. I never heard of that. Mine is *Impossible Charlie*."

"*I* never heard of *that*. Let's trade," I suggested.

"Great!"

I looked at my watch then. "Oh! I have to leave!" I cried. I explained about the test in a rush as Jessi and I ran downstairs. "Sorry I have to go," I said, "but bring your horse book to school tomorrow and I'll bring mine."

"Deal!" said Jessi happily. "You can see my toe shoes the next time you come over."

As I ran to the Kishis' house I felt as light as a bird. And I was full of confidence. Baby-sitting test? No sweat. I was ready for anything.

CHAPTER 5

As I had said, I wasn't sure who was going to give me the baby-sitting test. Maybe just Kristy and Claudia, or even Claudia by herself. But when I stepped into Claudia's room, I found all four girls there. They were sitting around pretty much like they had been the day before, and they were dressed pretty much like they had been the day before, but they looked very serious.

"Hi, Mallory," said Kristy from her director's chair. "Have a seat." She pointed to Claudia's desk. I noticed that it had been cleared off, except for a pad of blank paper and a couple of sharpened pencils.

I began to feel nervous, just like I do before a big test at school. What were they going to ask me?

Claudia's desk faced the wall, of course, but the chair had been turned around to face the room. I sat gingerly on the edge and pressed

41

my knees together. Kristy, Mary Anne, Dawn, and Claudia were looking at me gravely.

"Well," said Kristy. "I guess we better get started. The test is going to be in two parts — oral and drawing."

"Oral and drawing?" I repeated.

"Yes," said Claudia haughtily. "Oral means spoken."

I bet you anything in the world Claudia herself hadn't known the meaning of that word before today.

"I know it does," I replied quietly. "I was wondering about the drawing part. I'm not a bad artist, but —"

"Don't worry about that right now." Kristy brushed the problem away. "That's the second part of the test. First is the oral part."

"Okay." I folded my hands and bit my lip. I'm sure I was blushing.

"Now," began Kristy, "the thing about baby-sitting is that it's important to understand children —"

"Not just the kids you're sitting for," Dawn interrupted, "but children in general."

"Right," agreed Kristy briskly. "So it's important to know psychology and, um, child development." She paused. "*And* it's important to know how to handle any situation."

"Especially emergencies," said Mary Anne.

42

"Plus, you should know how to *prevent* problems and accidents."

I knew the girls were thinking about Nicky and his broken finger.

"Okay," I said slowly.

"So," said Kristy, "let's begin with the basics. Mary Anne, you get ready to keep score."

Mary Anne, who was sitting on the bed, opened the notebook to a blank page and poised a pen above the top line. "Ready," she told Kristy.

My heart was thumping along like horses' hoofs. I hoped nobody else could hear it. If the girls could hear it, they'd know I was nervous. And if they knew I was nervous, they might think it was because I didn't know much about baby-sitting and kids after all. Which wasn't true, of course.

Kristy cleared her throat. "At what age," she began, "does a baby cut his first tooth?"

I relaxed. That was easy. "Eight months," I replied.

"Wrong," said Kristy. She looked at Mary Anne. "Jot that down." She turned back to me. "It's seven months."

"But Claire cut her first two teeth when she was eight months old," I insisted. "I remember because —"

"Second question," said Kristy loudly. "Which

teeth does the baby usually cut first?"

"The middle ones on the bottom?" I guessed. Those had been the ones Claire had cut first, but maybe she wasn't normal or something.

"Are you asking us or telling us?" said Claudia.

"Um, telling you."

"Well, you're right," Kristy barked. "One point."

Whew.

"Third question," Kristy went on. "What is the difference between creeping and crawling?"

I almost replied, "Huh?" because I didn't know anything about creeping, except that my mother usually calls bugs "creepy things," or "creepy-crawlies," but I was pretty sure Kristy wasn't talking about bugs. However, I did know something about crawling.

"Um," I said, "well, see, crawling is how a baby gets around before he can walk. You know, on all fours."

"Wrong!" cried Kristy again. "Dawn, you want to explain the difference?"

"Crawling," said Dawn obediently, "is when a baby pulls himself along with his tummy on the ground. Creeping comes later and is done on all fours." She sounded as if she were reciting from a textbook.

What did this have to do with anything? I wondered.

"Let's move on to something else," said Kristy.

I breathed a sigh of relief.

Kristy had just opened her mouth to ask question number four, when Claudia's phone rang.

"I'll get it," said Claudia. No one else lunged for the phone. I guessed that was because the girls weren't having a meeting, so this was probably a private call for Claudia, not a job call.

Even so, we all listened to her end of the conversation. It sounded pretty exciting. After the "Hi's" and the "How are you's?" at the beginning, Claudia's face changed. "Really?" she shrieked. "No kidding? Oh, that's great! That's *great!*" There was a pause. "Oh, of course we're available. We'll change our schedules if we have to." She sounded fairly dignified by the time she said good-bye, but as soon as she hung up the phone, she began shrieking again and jumping up and down.

"Guess who that was!" she exclaimed.

"Who?" cried Kristy, Mary Anne, Dawn, and even I. I couldn't help it.

"Mr. Perkins. He was calling from the hospital. Mrs. Perkins had the baby this morning.

It's a girl and her name is Laura Elizabeth!"

With that, we *all* started shrieking and squealing and jumping around. The test was forgotten. I felt as if we were friends, instead of little me *versus* the four big baby-sitters. We were equal, and we were happy about an exciting event we'd been waiting for forever.

The Perkinses live right across the street from Claudia, in what was Kristy's house before she moved in with her stepfather. So we've only known the Perkinses for a few months, but they are the greatest family. They have two little girls — Myriah, who's almost six, and Gabbie Ann, who's almost three — and a dog named Chewbacca. Oh, also a cat named R.C. I've never sat for Myriah and Gabbie, but I see them around, and sometimes Claire or Margo plays with Myriah. Everyone likes the Perkinses, and for as long as we've known them, Mrs. Perkins has been pregnant. And now she had had another little girl.

All the club members began talking excitedly.

"Just think. Three girls," said Claudia.

"I helped Mrs. Perkins decorate the room," said Mary Anne.

"I wonder how much the baby weighs," said Claudia.

"I love the name Laura," said Kristy.

"Well," added Claudia, "Mr. Perkins is probably going to be needing extra sitters for Myriah and Gabbie during the next couple of weeks. First, while Mrs. Perkins is in the hospital, and then when she first gets home, because she'll be tired. Mallory and I are already signed up for Thursday afternoon, but, well, he said he'd call us at our meeting tomorrow to figure out some other times."

"Great," said Kristy. She sighed. "Another baby. I just love new babies. Remember when Lucy Newton was born?"

"Yeah," said Claudia and Mary Anne fondly. (Dawn didn't say anything. She hadn't known the Newtons then. But she did now. The Baby-sitters Club sits for Lucy and her big brother Jamie all the time.)

"Oh, well," said Kristy, snapping to attention. "Back to business."

Darn.

"We'll move on to the medical portion of the exam. Mallory, explain how and when to use a tourniquet."

"A tourniquet?"

"Yes."

I stared down at my hands. "Well, we've never had to use one at my house —"

"No excuse," said Kristy. "You might have to someday."

"But I was going to say," I went on, my

voice shaking, "that I think we learned about them in health class last year. They're — they're special bandages."

"Is that your complete answer?" Dawn wanted to know.

I nodded.

"I'll give her partial credit," said Mary Anne.

I was about to ask what the rest of the answer was, when Kristy said, "And when do you remove a tourniquet?"

"When, um, the bleeding has stopped?"

"Wrong again! *You* never take one off. You always let a doctor do it."

"No fair!" I exclaimed, surprising everyone in the room, including myself. "That was a trick question."

"Well," said Kristy huffily, "I hope you never put a tourniquet on *me*."

"Me, too," I muttered.

"Let's go on to the drawing part," Claudia urged Kristy nervously.

"All right," she agreed. "Turn around and sit at the desk, Mallory," said Kristy. "We want you to draw a picture of the human digestive system."

"*Why?*" I cried.

"Because it's an important thing to understand. You might have to sit for a kid with colic one day."

"If I do, I'll give him soy formula," I said. I was dangerously close to crying.

"Just draw."

My picture looked like this:

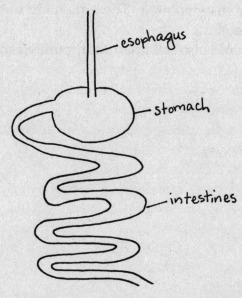

"Half credit," said Dawn, when I was finished. "She left out the liver, the gall bladder, the pancreas —"

"And about a hundred other things. *No* credit," said Kristy. "The test is over."

"But I didn't get to tell you guys what I *do* know," I protested.

"Come to the Friday club meeting and we'll discuss the results," Kristy said firmly. "Of *every*thing — since you and Claudia will be baby-sitting at the Perkinses' on Thursday. We'll have to see how you do there." She pulled her visor down over her eyes.

I could tell it was time for me to leave. I was really disappointed. The girls hadn't been fair to me at all.

I could also tell I had disappointed the girls.

CHAPTER 6

Today melory and I sat for the
Perkins. What an experyence! First
of all maria and Gaby were exited
aboat the new baby. So was I. I
love the idea of three litle grils!
And I love the name Laura Elzabeth.
Isn't that pretty! maria, Gaby and
Laura. I wish I had a baby sister.
melory has three yonger sisters
I guess that's why she didn't seem
to exited. Anyway heres how the
job whith melory went. not well.
It seemed like she'd never seen
a kid befor in her life....

I didn't read Claudia's poorly spelled note-book entry until a long time after she'd written it. When I did read it, I was mad. But I was mad at myself because Claudia was right. I was a *terrible* sitter that afternoon. Only I don't think it was all my fault. Claudia made me nervous.

I met Claudia in front of her house at 3:25 and we walked across the street to the Perkin-ses'. The door was answered by Mr. Perkins, Myriah, Gabbie, and Chewy. *Everyone* seemed excited, even Chewy. (Well, Chewy always does, so I don't know if this counts.)

Mr. Perkins, who was grinning widely, handed Claudia and me each a pink balloon. "In honor of Laura," he said.

"We have a baby! We have a baby sister!" cried Myriah, who was dancing around the front hall.

"Her name is Laura Elizabeth," added Gab-bie.

"I know. I think that's wonderful."

"I am so glad the baby is a girl," Gabbie went on. "Now she can wear all my old clothes."

I smiled at Gabbie and she smiled back.

"We visited the baby last night," Myriah

informed me. She was still jumping up and down. "We went to the hospital and we saw Mommy and Laura Beth. It was so, so fun."

"I've got to get going," said Mr. Perkins hurriedly. "I just came home to get Myriah at school and pick up Gabbie. She's been with friends of ours today. Now I'm going back to the hospital. Emergency numbers are in the kitchen near the phone. I guess you know everything else by now, Claudia. I'll put Chewy in the backyard on my way out. He can stay there." Mr. Perkins kissed Myriah and Gabbie. "I'll see you at dinnertime, girls. Tonight you can visit Mommy and your sister again. Maybe we'll go to Dunkin' Donuts on the way home."

"Dunkin' Donuts!" exclaimed Gabbie. "Oh, boy," she said as her father rushed off. "I love donuts! And the little donut holes, too. I want a chocolate donut. What are you going to get, Myriah?"

"Oh, I'm not sure," said Myriah. "I just want to see Laura Beth again. And Mommy. Hey, Claudia, don't you think Laura Beth is a good nickname for our baby?"

"It's great," agreed Claudia.

I decided I better show Claudia that I could take charge. "Are you guys hungry?" I asked Myriah and Gabbie.

"Starved," Myriah replied.

"Well, let's go have a snack. What do you want?"

"Cookies," said Gabbie.

"A Popsicle," said Myriah.

"Mallory," Claudia spoke up, sounding very superior, "It's usually better not to ask kids what they want. Just give them something — something healthy. That way, there won't be any arguments, and the parents will be happy, too. The girls are going to have donuts tonight. That's enough sweet stuff for one day."

"Oh, right," I said, my face reddening.

But I was annoyed. There was Ms. Junk-Food Junkie talking away about health food. And practically scolding me in front of Myriah and Gabbie.

I pretended I didn't care. And that I'd known what I was doing all along.

"Apples for everybody!" I called, trying to smile, as I led the girls into the kitchen.

"But we don't have any," Myriah said.

I looked in the fruit bowl and the refrigerator. She was right. There were no apples.

Claudia shook her head. Then she said, "Hey, you guys. Guess what you *do* have — bananas and raisins. You know what we can do with bananas and raisins?"

"What?" asked Myriah and Gabbie.

"We can make banana-men." Claudia peeled a banana and stuck raisins into it to give it eyes, a nose, and a mouth.

"Hey!" cried Myriah. "Cool! Can I eat it?"

"I want it!" said Gabbie.

"You can both have one," Claudia said. "We'll make another."

I felt completely left out. I might as well not have been there.

The afternoon didn't get much better. The next thing that happened was that I tried to pour a glass of milk for Gabbie and spilled it all over the kitchen counter. Then the glass slipped out of my hand and broke. Claudia had to take the girls out of the kitchen while I cleaned up the glass shards. Just as I was finishing, I heard Chewy scratching at the back door, so I let him in. After all, he'd been inside when I arrived.

Chewy tore into the house, tail whipping back and forth, and crashed his way into the living room, where he knocked three picture frames off a table with one sweep of his tail. Luckily, they didn't break.

"Mallory!" Claudia exclaimed. "What on earth?"

"Yikes! Chewy's a wildman!" Myriah shrieked.

"He was scratching at the door, so I let him

55

in," I said lamely. I made a grab for Chewy and missed his collar by inches.

"Mr. Perkins said to leave him outside," Claudia reminded me.

"Oh, yeah." Chewy rocked back on his haunches, stretching his front legs out, and barked playfully at me. "Come here, boy," I said. Chewy jumped away.

"I'll get him," said Myriah.

"And I'll help you," Claudia added. They dashed after Chewy as he headed into the dining room.

Gabbie and I looked at each other. Now what?

"Are you excited about seeing your mommy tonight? And your new sister?" I asked her.

Gabbie's eyes filled with tears and her chin quivered. "I miss Mommy," she said.

I sat on the couch and pulled Gabbie into my lap for a hug.

"What happened?" asked Claudia. She struggled into the living room, holding a wiggling, wagging Chewbacca by the collar.

"I said, 'Are you excited about seeing your mommy and your sister?' " I told Claudia, "and she started to cry. She misses her mother."

Claudia closed her eyes for a moment, as if I had made her so discombobulated that she had to stop and recover before she could do anything else. "All right," she went on. "Let me just take Chewy outside. Then I'll come back and straighten things out."

She would straighten things out?! No way. I could do it myself. First I tickled Gabbie and made faces until she began to giggle. Then I called Myriah into the living room and told the girls they were going to have a pajama party in the middle of the day. Claire and Margo like to do this sometimes.

I helped the Perkins girls into their night-clothes, and then the three of us gave each other new hairstyles and sang some songs.

Claudia looked somewhat happier.

Still, before the afternoon was over, I tripped while I was giving Myriah a piggyback ride and we fell down, and later I popped my Laura balloon, frightening both Gabbie and the cat.

I couldn't get home fast enough.

CHAPTER 7

"Please come to order," said Kristy primly, adjusting her visor. She looked around at the other people in the room. Mary Anne, Dawn, and Claudia were sitting side by side on Claudia's bed. I was sitting in the desk chair, the outcast.

It was Friday afternoon, five-thirty, the beginning of another meeting of the Baby-sitters Club.

"Have you all been reading the notebook?" asked Kristy.

"Yes," chorused Mary Anne, Dawn, and Claudia.

"How's the treasury?"

Dawn flipped through the record book. "Fine. This week's dues helped. If we don't spend anything for awhile, then no problem."

"Okay," said Kristy. "In that case, the next — and most important — order of business is

Mallory's test. And Mallory herself." She glanced at me.

I glanced back and tried to smile. I know my smile was wobbly.

"Mallory," said Kristy, "you flunked the test." She said it flat-out like that, but she didn't sound mean. She sounded disappointed and a little sorry for me.

"It was a hard test," I said.

"We know. It was supposed to be. Baby-sitting is serious business."

"But the test wasn't fair."

"Fair?" cried Kristy. "Wait a second. We're not talking about fair here. We're talking about children. What if you were baby-sitting and one of the kids was in a bicycle accident and was bleeding really, really badly?"

"I'd dial nine-one-one. I'd call for an ambulance or the police."

"And then what? What would you do while you were waiting for help?"

"I — I'm not sure. I'd have to see what was going on."

"And *really*," said Claudia. "Your drawing of the divestive system was terrible."

"*Dig*estive system," I corrected her.

Claudia blushed. I actually felt good that I'd made her do that.

"Furthermore," said Kristy, "what if you were sitting for a seven-month-old baby who was crying and crying and you did everything you could think of — maybe even gave it *soy formula* for colic — when the real problem was that the baby was teething? Only that didn't occur to you because you think babies don't cut their first teeth until they're *eight* months old?"

"But I wouldn't give a baby soy formula if the mother didn't tell me to!"

Luckily, the phone rang then. The girls forgot about me and the test as Mary Anne took the call and made a sitting appointment for Dawn. The caller must have been a new client because Mary Anne kept telling her (or him) things like, "Yes, we meet three times a week — Monday, Wednesday, and Friday afternoons from five-thirty until six. . . . No, our going rate is a little higher than that. . . . We're available weekends, evenings, and afternoons."

But as soon as Mary Anne hung up the phone, Kristy turned to Claudia and said, "On a scale of one to ten, how would you rate Mallory's job with the Perkins girls yesterday?"

"On a scale of one to ten?" Claudia repeated.

"Yes. One being lousy, five being average,

and ten being so incredibly wonderful you almost can't believe it."

"Mmm . . . a three," said Claudia.

"A *three!*" I exclaimed.

"Well, let's face it Mallory, you spilled milk, broke a glass, and had a complete disaster with the dog."

"But those were accidents," I protested. "Most of them."

"Then there was the business with the snack."

"What was that?" asked Dawn.

Claudia told the story about the apples and her stupid banana-men.

"You made me nervous!" I finally accused her. "You watched me like a hawk and you criticized everything I did!"

The phone rang again. Dawn answered it. Mr. Perkins was calling. They talked for several minutes, lining up appointments.

"How's the baby?" Kristy called from the director's chair.

"How's the baby?" Dawn asked Mr. Perkins. "Oh, good. . . . Thanks! I'll tell Claudia. She'll be glad to hear that. Yeah, she had fun yesterday, too."

What about me? I thought. Dawn was talking as if only Claudia had baby-sat. I was there with her. Didn't she think I counted? I guess not, since I'd been responsible for all those accidents.

As soon as Dawn hung up the phone, the girls began talking excitedly about babies.

"Remember when Lucy Newton was born?" asked Claudia. "Remember her colic?"

"Yeah, that was terrible," said Mary Anne.

"She cried endlessly," added Kristy.

"Claire had colic," I spoke up.

"Oh, yeah. You mentioned that," replied Claudia. "I don't think the Newtons gave Lucy soy sauce, though, like you did."

"I *hope* not!" I exclaimed. "Soy sauce!"

"Huh?" said Claudia.

At last, I thought. Something I really knew about — that the girls didn't know much about at all.

"Soy *sauce*," I said, "is a salty, um, condiment. For your food. Soy *formula* is a very gentle formula to give to babies who have trouble with milk. I should know."

The girls were looking at me. I felt like saying, "Nyah, nyah-nyah, nyah, nyah. I know something you don't know."

"Oh," said Claudia in a small voice.

Silence reigned.

Then Kristy said, "When are Mrs. Perkins and the baby coming home?"

Dawn cleared her throat. "Tomorrow," she replied.

"Oh, wow. That's wonderful!" cried Mary Anne.

"Let's celebrate," added Claudia. "Now let's see. Where —"

"Do you still have Gummi Worms in your hollow book?" asked Kristy hopefully.

"Sure." Claudia pulled a fat book off her shelf. She opened the cover. To my surprise, there were no pages inside, just a hollowed-out space. And the hole was filled with a mess of squiggly Gummi Worms.

Claudia handed one to each of us. The girls raised their worms in the air. I raised mine, too.

"To Laura Elizabeth Perkins," said Kristy. And she bit into her worm.

The rest of us ate our worms, too, except for Dawn, who just played with hers. "Not only are these worms junk food," she said, "but they're disgusting. I personally do not see how you guys can eat worm heads."

We began to giggle.

"Once," I spoke up, "when Nicky was really little, he ate part of a mudpie."

"Oh, gross!" cried Mary Anne.

"My brother once ate dog food," said Kristy.

"He thought it was leftover hamburger."

"Ew, ew, ew!" said Mary Anne.

The phone rang and the girls lined up a couple of sitting jobs. It was almost six o'clock. Time for the meeting to end.

Even so, Dawn said, "The Barretts' dog once ate a knee sock."

We began to laugh again.

"Remember when we were at Sea City," Mary Anne said to me, "and I got sunburned and Claire brought me a tub of margarine to rub on my skin?"

We laughed harder. *This* was how I usually thought of the girls in the Baby-sitters Club — nice, funny people who like to have a good time (but who are also serious sitters, of course).

Since we seemed so relaxed, I dared to say, "Well, it's almost time to go home. Um . . . have you decided whether I can be in the club?"

Kristy sighed. She got out of the director's chair and crossed the room to the bed, where she had a huddle with the other girls. When they were done talking, Kristy turned to me. "You can be in the club if you pass another test."

"*Another* test?" I couldn't believe it. How dare they? One unfair test wasn't enough?

"You flunked the first one," said Kristy mildly.

"It . . . was . . . NOT . . . *FAIR!*"

"Was too."

"*Was not!*" Kristy must be crazy.

"Then you can't be in the club."

"Don't worry," I told her, jumping angrily to my feet. "I'm not going to be in your stupid club. I quit!"

"You haven't joined yet!" Kristy yelled as I stomped out of the room.

"That's the best thing that's happened to me all year!" I yelled back. Then I ran home.

CHAPTER 8

There are a lot of things I do well, and one of them is mope. I moped all weekend and I moped through school Monday morning. At noon, I ate my lunch quickly, then escaped to the playground. Way off in a far corner of the playground is this fat, comforting sycamore tree. That's where I headed.

I walked slowly to it, dragging my feet with every step. When I reached the tree, I plopped down and leaned against its trunk. The tree is so huge you can only reach your arms about halfway around it. I wondered how old the tree was. I wondered how long the playground had been near it. I wondered how many other kids had sat by the tree or cried by it or even talked to it when they were upset.

While I wondered about these things, I felt around on the ground for a good worry stone, something smooth to play with while I brooded.

I ran my hand through the pebbles until it met . . . another hand!

A brown hand was lying near mine. It jumped when I touched it.

"Aughhh!" I shrieked.

"Aughhh!" shrieked the person attached to the hand.

I scrambled to my feet and could tell someone else was scrambling to his or her feet on the other side of the tree. After a moment I dared to peek around the trunk. I found myself face to face with Jessi Ramsey.

"Oh, it's only you," we exclaimed at the same time.

Then we had to hook pinkies and say "jinx."

We sighed and slid back to the ground. This time we sat next to each other.

"I read *Impossible Charlie*," I told Jessi. "It was great. Really funny."

"And I read *A Morgan for Melinda*," she replied. "That was great, too."

"Let's switch back and then switch two more books. I've got one called *The Lightning Time*. It reminds me of *The Lion, the Witch and the Wardrobe*. You know, from the *Narnia Chronicles*."

"Oh, yeah? I've got all seven Narnia books."

"You do? I'll trade you *The Lightning Time*

for the *The Horse and His Boy*. I read every Narnia book except that one."

"Okay."

I looked at the ground. I still needed a worry stone. Jessi was looking at the ground, too.

"Everything all right?" I asked her.

She shrugged. "How about you?"

I shrugged.

"Do you come to this tree a lot?" Jessi wanted to know.

"Only to mope."

Jessi nodded. "It seems like a good moping place."

"Yeah."

"I'm so mopey I can't even think of any good jokes. How come *you're* moping?"

I paused, trying to decide whether to tell Jessi about my problem. She looked as if another problem were the last thing she needed. Finally I decided that telling her about it wouldn't make it her problem. It would still be mine. All she had to do was listen. And I'd be willing to listen to her problem, if she had one.

"Well," I began, "remember that baby-sitting test I told you about?"

Jessi nodded.

"I flunked it."

"Oh, wow. That's too bad. I'm really sorry."

"Me, too. But the thing is, it wasn't a fair

test. Listen to some of the questions they asked me: When does a baby cut his first tooth? What's the difference between creeping and crawling?''

"Huh?" said Jessi.

"That's what I thought. Then they asked me to explain how and when to use a tourniquet. And *then* they told me to draw a picture of the human digestive system."

"You are kidding!"

"Nope. All I could remember was the esophagus, the stomach, and the intestines."

"Ew," said Jessi. Then she added, "What else is there?"

"Oh, the liver, the pancreas, and a bunch of other organs. But it doesn't matter. You know what the worst part was?"

"What?"

"That I didn't fit in with those girls. I thought we could be friends. After all, I know them pretty well. But I was dressed all wrong at the first meeting, and I was really nervous when I went on this trial baby-sitting job with one of the girls. . . . Oh, it's just a big mess. And I don't belong."

"Tell me about it," said Jessi bitterly. "At least the only place you don't belong is in that club. I don't belong in this school, or even this *town*. Neither does my family."

"You mean because you're, um . . ."

"You can say it," Jessi told me. "Because we're black."

"Have people done things to you?" I asked.

"Nope." Jessi shook her head. "Well, a few things. Like Benny Ott shooting rubber bands at me in class. And I've overheard Rachel Robinson and her friends talking about me. Mostly, though, it's what they *haven't* done. The neighbors haven't said hello to my family, haven't introduced themselves to us, haven't paid any attention to us. Except my dad. His company *asked* him to take his job, so the people he works with are okay. But, well, do you know you're the only kid in school who talks to me? I mean, *to* me, not *about* me behind my back."

"I am?"

Jessi nodded. "No one talks to Becca, either."

"Wow."

"I'm even thinking of not taking dancing lessons here. I don't know if it's worth it. Can't you just imagine it? They'd hold auditions for a ballet, and I'd try out, but they'd never give me the lead, even if I were as good as Pavlova."

"Who's Pavlova?"

"This famous ballerina. You know what would happen if they *did* give me the lead?"

"What?" I asked.

"Everyone would be upset that a black girl got it instead of a white girl."

"I guess," I said slowly.

"I *know*."

"What was it like where you used to live"

"In New Jersey? Oh, really different. For one thing, there were lots of black families in Oakley. And our neighborhood was all black. Well, our street was, anyway."

"Where your relatives lived?"

"Yup. Grandma and Grandpa next door. Keisha, Kara, and Billy across the street. Sandy and Molly down the block, and Raun and Isaac down the block in the other direction. Plus lots of friends."

"And your ballet class?"

"Half black kids, half white kids. Well, maybe more blacks than whites. Last year, you know what?"

"What?"

"We put on *The Nutcracker Suite* and the lead parts were all played by black students. I got to be Clara."

"Oh, lucky!"

"Yeah . . . my costume was beautiful."

"I bet."

"We have pictures."

"Can I see them sometime?" I asked.

"Sure."

"You know, Jessi, you must have been really good to get the part of Clara," I said.

"Well, Clara's role isn't really the hardest. I think it's just the most important, because the story is Clara's dream. But I *am* good. Mama and Daddy say I'm crazy not to take lessons here. I mean, because of my reason. If I wanted to stop because I had too much homework or so that I could have time to try something else, that would be different. It would be a good reason. But my parents say black people and white people live in the same world so they better get along. And if I don't take dance because I don't want to compete with white kids, then I'm being chicken."

I thought about that. "Still," I said, "it doesn't seem fair. And it's awful not to belong. The funny thing is, I never thought I didn't belong until I wanted to be in the Baby-sitters Club."

"And *I* never thought *I* didn't belong until we moved to Stoneybrook," said Jessi.

"Maybe *we're* not the problem," I said. "Maybe everyone else is."

"Yeah!"

I sighed. "But that doesn't change things. I'm still not in the club. And I want to baby-sit. I love kids. I have seven younger brothers and sisters."

"Seven! Wow."

"And I'm good with them. I know I am."

"I love kids, too," said Jessi. "Mama says I'm like Squirt's second mother. And in Oakley my aunt Yvonne let me baby-sit for Kara sometimes. Kara's two. And four times I got *paid* to baby-sit for this little kid named Chelsea. She's three."

"Last summer the girls in the Baby-sitters Club ran a playgroup and they let me help them. They didn't think I was a baby then, and I didn't make mistakes, either."

I had given up searching for a worry stone. I didn't need one now that I was talking with Jessi.

"I bet we're both really good baby-sitters," said Jessi.

"Yeah," I agreed, sounding almost angry. Then I glanced at Jessi. I think she and I got the same idea at the same time. "Hey!" I cried. "Let's do it! Let's start our own baby-sitting club."

"Just us," said Jessi, grinning. "The best eleven-year-old sitters anywhere!"

"No, the best *any-age* sitters."

"Right."

"I know we can do it," I said.

"I'm sure of it."

"We don't need the Baby-sitters Club."

"Especially if they don't need you."

"Yeah."

When the bell rang, Jessi and I stood up together and ran to the school building. I couldn't wait to begin our own club. I was really excited. So was Jessi. Maybe we didn't belong with some people, but we belonged with each other.

CHAPTER 9

That afternoon, Jessi walked home from school with me.

Claire greeted us as soon as we reached my house. She was waiting in the front yard and dashed across the lawn when she saw us. Claire goes to morning kindergarten, so she gets home a couple of hours before my brothers and sisters and I do. She's always glad to see us.

"Hi! Hi, Mallory!" she called. Then she stopped short and looked Jessi up and down. "Who are you?" she asked.

Please, please, Claire, I thought. Don't say anything embarrassing.

Before Jessi could answer, Claire went on, "Hey, did you come to cl —"

And all at once I knew what she was going to say. She was going to say, "Did you come to clean our house?" That was because Claire had seen only a few black people in her life.

Recently, two black women had shown up when my mom called the Fast 'n' Easy Cleaning Service in Stamford, needing help getting ready for a party.

Before Claire could finish her sentence I jumped in and said loudly, "This is Jessi Ramsey. She's my new friend from school. Jessi, this is Claire, my youngest sister."

"Hi," said Jessi. She knelt down to Claire's level. "You look like you lost a tooth."

It was just the right thing to say.

Claire smiled a gap-toothed smile. "I did! Two days ago. And I put it under my pillow and the tooth fairy took it away — and left twenty-five cents!"

"Wow," exclaimed Jessi. "You are lucky!"

"I keep my teeth in a box that looks like a tooth. The dentist gave it to me."

Claire and Jessi were still talking about teeth when Margo, Nicky, and Vanessa came home. I knew the triplets wouldn't be far behind, unless they were staying at school for soccer practice.

I braced myself, wondering if I'd have to field any more embarrassing questions, but the kids didn't seem too surprised by Jessi. And she was great with them. She kept asking all the right questions.

"Wow," she said to Nicky. "What happened to your hand?"

That started Nicky's long story of his broken finger. He'd told it lots of times by then, and each time, the story grew a little.

"The doctor said it was the *worst* broken finger he *ever saw.*"

"Oh, Nicky, he did not," said Vanessa.

"Yes, he did. He said it was broken in seventeen places."

"Two," I whispered to Jessi.

"And this cast weighs twelve pounds."

"One," I whispered. "At most."

Jessi grinned.

"Let's go inside, you guys," I said. "I'm hungry."

We ran into our kitchen and my brothers and sisters began opening drawers and pawing through the refrigerator. They pulled out bread and baloney and mustard, Twinkies and Oreos and Yodels, apples and bananas and oranges.

"Mom," I said, as my mother watched the chaos, "this is Jessi. She moved into Stacey McGill's house."

My mother looked just a teeny tiny bit surprised, but she held out her hand and shook Jessi's. "Welcomé to the neighborhood," she said.

"Thanks," replied Jessi. She sounded both pleased and surprised.

"Help yourselves to a snack," offered Mom.

I glanced around the kitchen. Nicky was awkwardly lathering mustard onto baloney slices, rolling them up, and biting into them, making the mustard ooze out the other end. Margo was untwisting Oreos, scraping out the filling, and saving it in a pile to eat after she'd eaten the cookie parts. Claire was a sticky mess from a banana, and Vanessa was grinning at everyone with an orange peel stuck in her mouth.

"We'll eat upstairs," I told my mother.

She nodded understandingly.

Jessi and I each took an apple and a cookie and went to my room.

"Oops," said Jessi as soon as we were sitting on my bed. "I better call Mom and tell her where I am."

She called her from the phone in the hall and then came back into my room. "You sure do have a lot of books," she said, looking around.

"They're Vanessa's and mine. She shares the room with me. That shelf is hers, this one is mine," I told her, pointing.

Jessi stood in front of my shelf. "Horse stories," she murmured. "Fantasy, mystery. I see lots of books I'd like to borrow. You and I could switch back and forth forever. It would be like having our own library."

"Yeah!" I said. "I like that idea."

Jessi sat next to me on the bed. "So," she said, "how do we start a baby-sitting club?"

"Well, let me tell you how the other club works. We can sort of copy it. The girls meet three times a week from five-thirty until six. And the people they sit for know they meet at those times, so they call during the meetings and say when they need sitters. The good thing is that when people call — the baby-sitters call them clients — they're almost guaranteed a sitter, since they've reached four people at once. *Some*body is bound to be free."

"Oh, I see," said Jessi.

"So the sitter takes down the information about the job; you know, how many kids they'll be in charge of, how old they are, how long the parents will be away, stuff like that. Then Mary Anne Spier — she's the secretary — looks in their appointment book to find out who's free, and when they figure out who's going to take the job, they call the client back with the information.

"They get millions of jobs that way. They're always busy. The parents around here really like them," I added wistfully. No matter how

79

hurt I was, I still wanted to be part of the Baby-sitters Club.

"Hmm," said Jessi. "Well, I don't see why we can't do that, too. There seem to be lots of kids around here. The Baby-sitters Club can't handle everything."

"You're right about that. That's why they asked me to join. They need someone to replace Stacey, I mean, *really* need someone."

"Well . . . let's get to work!" said Jessi. "First, we'll pick out a name for our club. I think the Baby-sitters Club is a dumb name. It's too plain. It's like naming a restaurant The Restaurant."

I giggled. "Yeah. Those older girls don't have any imagination. We could call our club . . . um . . ."

"Yeah. We could call it . . . um . . ."

We found that it wasn't easy to think of a better name.

"How about Sitters United?" suggested Jessi.

I shook my head. "Nah . . . How about, um, Sitters Incorporated?"

Jessi shook her head. "Nah. Boring. . . . Hmm. . . . Hey, how about Kids Incorporated?"

"Yeah!" I cried. "That's great! It sounds really cute. It's catchy."

"Much catchier than the Baby-sitters Club."

"Right."

"Now what?"

"Well, the other girls are always advertising themselves. Last year they put an ad in the newspaper, and every now and then they print up fliers and stick them in people's mailboxes, just to remind them of the club."

"Okay. Let's make fliers. . . . How do we do that?"

I thought for a moment. "My brother has a toy printing press that really works. I bet he'd let us use it."

"Great."

I leaned out into the hall and yelled, "Hey, Byron!"

"The triplets aren't home from school yet, Mallory," my mother called.

"Darn," I said. "We need to use his printing press. For something really important. Do you think he'd let us?"

"We-ell," said Mom. She likes to let us kids solve our own problems, so she doesn't barge into situations that don't concern her. But at last she said, "That printing press has been stuck up in the attic for over a year now. Byron never uses it, so I'll give you permission. If he gets upset, he can get upset with me."

"Oh, *thanks*, Mom!" I cried.

I retrieved the printing press from the attic

and brought it into my room. "Here it is," I said to Jessi. "Now we just have to figure out how to use it."

"And what to say on the fliers."

"Oh, yeah," I replied. "Right. Well, I guess we say when we're available to sit."

"After school," said Jessi. "Weekends."

"How about at night?"

Jessi shook her head. "I don't think I'm allowed to."

"Me neither. Unless I'm sitting right here at home."

"I wonder if anyone will really hire us. We *are* only eleven."

"I'm sure they'd hire us if we sat together. Two baby-sitters for the price of one."

"Yeah!" cried Jessi. "And that's what we should put on the fliers!"

So we did.

Setting up the printing press wasn't easy. The first flier read: Two sitters for eht brice oi one. But we kept working. When we had a good flier we ran off thirty copies. We paid Nicky and Vanessa twenty-five cents each to put the fliers in the mailboxes on our street and on Jessi's.

While they were doing that, I said, "Let's make a few phone calls. It can't hurt to *tell* people what we're doing. I could call Mrs.

Barrett. She lives right down the street and has three kids. I know them really well. And I could call Jenny Prezzioso's mom, and maybe Jamie Newton's mother."

We had just finished our phoning when we heard a knock on the door. Mom stuck her head in the room. "Is this the headquarters of Kids Incorporated?" she asked.

"Yes," I replied, wondering what was coming.

"Well, I'd like to hire you for Saturday afternoon."

"Okay, great," I said calmly.

Jessi and I waited until Mom had left before we began screaming and jumping up and down. "Our first job!" I shrieked. "Our first job!"

Kids Incorporated seemed to be off to a good start.

CHAPTER 10

Uh-oh, you guys. I smell trouble.
I mean, there is trouble and by
now we're all aware of it, since
I've called you. But just so we have
it on record, I'll write up the incident
here in our notebook.

As you know it started when I
went to the Barretts' house to sit for
Marnie and Suzi. (Buddy was off
visiting his dad.) The girls were fine,
as usual. Sometimes they can be
a handful, but they're never really
bad. Anyway, after I had discovered
Suzi taping diapers around table
legs, I decided it was time to go
outside and take a walk. We put
Pow on his leash and had gotten
as far as the Pikes' house when
I saw it: Trouble....

Dawn's sitting job at the Barretts' house was on a Saturday afternoon — the same afternoon that Mom had hired Jessi and me to sit for my brothers and sisters. I didn't know just what had happened on Dawn's job until a few weeks later when I read her notebook entry and asked her some questions. This is what I found out:

Dawn arrived at the Barretts' at two o'clock. The house was looking neater than usual because Mrs. Barrett had finally found a woman to help her with the cleaning. For a long time she'd been trying to juggle a job with being both mother and father to Buddy, Suzi, and Marnie. (The Barretts are divorced.) She hadn't had enough time to do *any*thing right, so when Dawn first met them, their house was a mess and the kids were a worse mess.

But now things are better. Mrs. Barrett has become more organized. Before she left that day, she even remembered to tell Dawn where the emergency numbers are, that Marnie would be getting up from her nap around two-thirty, and that Suzi had a slight earache and needed medicine at three o'clock.

The afternoon started off quietly. Dawn and Suzi (who's four) built a playground out of Legos for Suzi's stuffed animals. They were just putting on the finishing touches when

Dawn heard Marnie calling from upstairs. Sometimes when she wakes up from a nap, she cries. Other times, she talks or sings. That afternoon she was calling, "Hi-ho, hi-ho, hi-ho! . . . Grape juice. Grape juice, please? . . . Hi-ho, hi-ho, hi-ho."

"Marnie's up," Dawn told Suzi. "I'm going to change her and bring her downstairs. I'll be back in a few minutes."

Dawn ran up to Marnie's room. She pushed the door open slowly and said, "Hi, Marnie-o," in a soft voice. (It's never a good idea to barge in on a kid who's just woken up from a nap, especially since the kid might be expecting to see her mommy and not a baby-sitter.) Marnie was in a great mood that day. She wrinkled her nose up into the "ham face" she makes when she's happy. Then she began to jump up and down in her crib, her blonde curls bouncing. "Hi-ho, hi-ho!" she called.

"Hi-ho!" Dawn replied. "Boy, are you a happy little girl today."

"Hi-ho," Marnie said again. (Marnie's not even two years old yet.)

"Time to change your diaper," Dawn said, picking Marnie up and carrying her to the changing table. She reached into the box of disposable diapers that was next to the table and pulled out the last one. Uh-oh, she thought, but then she remembered that Mrs. Barrett usually keeps a big supply of diapers in the laundry room.

"No-no. No didy," said Marnie.

"Yes-yes. Sorry, kiddo," Dawn told her. "You're soaking wet."

Dawn sang "Baa, Baa, Black Sheep" to Marnie as she changed the diaper, and Marnie made the ham face again. Then Dawn snapped her into a pair of clean overalls, picked her up, and carried her downstairs.

"Suzi?" she called. "Do you want to have some juice with Marnie?"

No answer.

Dawn peered into the playroom.

Suzi wasn't there.

"Suzi!" Dawn called more loudly.

"What?" replied Suzi's voice.

"Where are you?"

"In the dining room."

Dawn carried Marnie into the dining room. She didn't know what she expected to find there — but it certainly wasn't the sight of Suzi wrapping diapers around the legs of the table and taping them in place with Band-Aids.

"What are you doing?!" exclaimed Dawn.

"Fixing my horsie," Suzi replied. She opened another Band-Aid wrapper, expertly peeled off the paper, and applied the Band-Aid to the edges of a diaper, securing it just under the tabletop.

"Excuse me?" said Dawn.

Suzi patted the table. "My horsie broke all his legs," she said. "And he has a sickness. I have to fix him up."

Dawn clapped her hand to her forehead. Then she set Marnie on the ground. "Suzi, your mom needs these diapers for your sister. I'm, um, I'm really glad you made your horse better, but now we have to take the Band-Aids off — carefully. Try to do it without ruining the diapers."

It took almost fifteen minutes, but at last the diapers had been unwound from the table, folded neatly, and placed in their box in the laundry room. Dawn might not have been so concerned if she didn't know how expensive disposable diapers are.

She decided it was definitely time to get the girls outdoors, so after a quick snack, and after she'd given Suzi her medicine, she put Pow on his leash, walked the girls into the garage, and plopped Marnie in her stroller.

"Where are we walking to?" asked Suzi as they headed down the driveway. "The school playground?"

"We-ell, that's kind of a long walk, but I guess we could try."

"Wait! Could we go to the brook?" asked Suzi. "Marnie loves it."

"Sure," replied Dawn. "That's a great idea. And the brook is much closer."

Dawn, Suzi, and Marnie hadn't walked far when suddenly Dawn saw something that made her stop short. She stopped so quickly that Pow, whose leash was attached to the stroller and who was trotting happily ahead, jerked to a halt, too, and nearly fell over.

What Dawn had seen was *me*. Well, not just me, but Jessi and me across the street with all of my brothers and sisters.

Dawn told me later that her first thought was, why are *they* baby-sitting? Her second thought was, maybe they're not sitting, maybe they're just playing with the kids. Then she noticed that my parents' cars weren't in the driveway and knew we were sitting after all.

"Wow," said Dawn under her breath. Of course, she was dying of curiosity. If Mrs. Pike needed another sitter, why hadn't she called the Baby-sitters Club? She always had before. And furthermore, who was the girl who was helping me baby-sit (if that's what she was doing)?

Dawn had a lot of unanswered questions, but she wasn't going to ask *me* about them. It was embarrassing enough that we'd seen each other. I hadn't spoken to any of the girls in the club since I'd marched out of Claudia's room announcing I was "quitting."

Unfortunately, Suzi didn't know any of this.

"Dawn?" she said. "Can I go play with Claire?"

Dawn bit her lip. She hated to say no just because she and I were having problems. Why should Suzi and Claire suffer for that? Finally she said, "Don't you want to go to the brook? We can throw stones in the water and float leaves under the bridge. Hey, we can play Poohsticks just like Winnie-the-Pooh and his friends do in *The House at Pooh Corner*. We might even see some squirrels there. Or a rabbit." Dawn was pulling out all the stops.

"Maybe we'll see a snake!" Suzi cried excitedly. Her decision was made. Dawn felt relieved — especially because Suzi hadn't yelled across the street to ask Claire to join them.

So Dawn took the girls to the brook and they did toss stones and float leaves and play Poohsticks. And they saw a squirrel, which Pow chased joyfully. (They did *not* see any snakes.) When they returned to the Barretts' house later, Dawn was still wondering about Jessi and me and whether we were baby-sitting. And why. And who Jessi was.

Her questions were answered not long after when she was getting more juice for Marnie. She opened the refrigerator and for the first time noticed something tacked to the door with a magnet shaped like a frog. It was one of our fliers for Kids Incorporated. It listed Jessi's name and my name, our ages, phone numbers, and the club meeting times. (Jessi and I had decided to run the club just the way the Baby-sitters Club was run. We'd even bought an appointment book and a notebook.)

Dawn finished her sitting job in a huff. As soon as she got home, she called Kristy with the news. She figured that, as president, Kristy ought to hear it first.

"Guess what," Dawn said flatly.

"What?" replied Kristy. "Boy, you sound like you're in a good mood."

"I'm in a rotten mood and it's all because of what I have to tell you. Mallory Pike has started her own baby-sitting club."

"What?!" screeched Kristy. "How could she? Who else is in the club?"

"Some girl named Jessi Ramsey. She's new here. I think she's the one whose family moved into Stacey's house."

"Hmphh," was all Kristy would reply. After a pause she added, "Well, who'll hire them?

They're too young. They won't get any jobs. . . . And Mallory doesn't know the first thing about tourniquets."

"Mrs. Pike already hired them," Dawn informed her. "They were sitting there this afternoon when I was at the Barretts'. That's how I know about all this."

"The Pikes! They're practically our best customers," moaned Kristy. "Mallory can't do this to us."

"Well, she is doing it."

"Hmphh," said Kristy again. "Well, I'll just get on the phone with Mary Anne and Claudia. This absolutely cannot happen."

"How are you going to stop it?" I asked.

"I don't know," replied Kristy. "I really don't know."

CHAPTER 11

"The second meeting of Kids Incorporated will now come to order," I said.

It was Monday afternoon, five-thirty. Not far away, the girls in the Baby-sitters Club were holding a meeting of their own. I wondered if Claudia's phone had rung yet. I decided that it might have, since it seemed to ring an awful lot.

The girls in the Baby-sitters Club held their meetings with the door closed. Jessi and I had to hold ours with the door open so we could hear the phone in the hall. We'd set it on the floor, as close to the doorway as the cord would stretch, but it was *not* the same as having my own phone. Plus, my brothers and sisters ran upstairs every two seconds.

I looked at Jessi. "This is not exactly like the Baby-sitters Club," I told her.

"No?"

I explained about the phone and the privacy.

"And another thing," I added. "They have club officers. You know, president, vice-president, secretary, treasurer. But there are only two of us."

"You could be the president," said Jessi, "since you know how to run a baby-sitting club."

"But you thought of the great name for our club," I pointed out.

Jessi frowned. "Let's not have officers," she said. "Let's be equal."

"Okay," I agreed. "We can take turns with everything — answering the phone, writing down appointments."

"Perfect."

We sat and waited for the phone to ring.

It didn't.

"I guess it takes a while for things to get started," said Jessi.

"I guess."

"What do the other girls do when they're not on the phone?"

"Gossip," I replied. "Talk about boys."

"Ew," said Jessi. "Boys."

"I know. Ew. We could gossip, though."

"About who?"

"Benny Ott."

"He's a boy!"

"No, he isn't. He isn't even human."

Jessi laughed. "Well, I've got some news to tell you. I didn't want to say anything until I knew for sure, but last week I decided that I would take ballet lessons here after all."

"That's great!" I cried.

"Thanks," said Jessi, and ducked her head, looking embarrassed. "We called this ballet school in Stamford," she went on, "and they asked me to come in and audition."

"Did you?"

"Yup."

"And what happened? Oh, this is so exciting!"

"Well . . ." said Jessi slowly.

"Don't keep me in suspense!"

"I got in! To the advanced class! And everyone was *super* nice."

"Oh, wow! That is wonderful! Really. Boy, just think of it. I know a real live dancer. Is your school going to put on a ballet soon?"

"Well, *The Nutcracker*, of course, at Christmastime, but before that, I think we have some kind of recital. Parts of *Swan Lake* and other ballets, but not an actual ballet like you're thinking of."

"Can I come see you at Christmas?"

"Of course, if I'm in the ballet."

"You will be. I just know it. I can feel it."

Jessi smiled at me. "Thanks, Mal," she said.

"You know, you're a real friend, a true friend. I didn't think I'd find another true friend after I moved away from Keisha, but I did. I found you."

"This is getting mushy," I said, but I was smiling, too. Maybe Jessi really was going to become my best friend. My first best friend. It felt awfully nice to be sitting in my room, telling each other important things and making each other smile.

The moment was ruined, though, by the sound of feet thundering up the stairs. Above the noise of the feet were shouts of, "Give it! That's mine!"

"It is not!"

"Is too!"

"Is NOT!"

"YES. IT. IS. Give it!"

I ran into the hallway and found Nicky and Margo tusseling over a green plastic toy.

"Break it up, you guys," I said firmly.

My brother and sister separated, shooting looks at each other that were as lethal as darts.

"You know," I said quietly, taking the toy out of Margo's hand. "This thing is one of the triplets' Wandering Frog People. It doesn't belong to either of you."

"But —" began Margo.

"But —" began Nicky.

I silenced them by holding up one hand. "I am now going to put this in the triplets' room. Then I order you to go downstairs and catch a dinosaur."

Nicky and Margo looked at each other and began to giggle. Then they clattered down the stairs together.

Jessi smiled as I came back into the bedroom. "You really handled that well," she told me.

"Thanks," I replied. "I just wish the girls in the Baby-sitters Club could have seen it."

"Well, you don't need them now," Jessi told me. "We've got Kids Incorporated."

"Right."

And just then the phone rang. A job call! "Aughh! I'll get it!" I shrieked. I leaped off my bed and ran into the hall. Then I picked up the phone very sedately. "Hello, Kids Incorporated. . . . Oh, okay. Hang on a sec." I put the phone down. "It's for Vanessa," I whispered to Jessi. Then I yelled down the stairs, "VANESSA! PHONE! And don't stay on too long."

I went back to my room. While we waited for Vanessa to get off the phone, Jessi told me two jokes. One went like this:

Q: What does it mean when you see an elephant walking down the street in a blue shirt?

A: It means his red one is in the wash.

(I knew that one already.) The other joke went like this:

Q: What's black and white and black and white and black and white and black and white?

A: A zebra rolling down a hill.

(I didn't know that one, and it made me giggle.) "I'll have to tell it to my brothers and sisters," I said.

The phone rang again. "Oh, thank goodness Vanessa's off," I cried.

"Can I get it?" asked Jessi.

"Of course," I replied.

"Hello, Kids Incorporated. May I help you?" Jessi said professionally when she'd picked up the phone. "Oh, hi, Mama." Jessi made a face at me as if to say, "It's only my *mother*," but then she went on, "Oh, really? Sure. . . . Okay. Thanks, Mama. 'Bye." She hung up. "Guess what!" she exclaimed as she bounced back into the room. "Mama just hired us! She needs us to watch Becca and Squirt next Wednesday afternoon while she has her hair done."

"Fantastic!" I cried, and wrote the job in our appointment book.

No sooner had I done that than the phone rang again. "I'll get this one," I said to Jessi. "Wow, busy day."

I sat on the floor in the hall and picked up

the phone. "Hello, Kids Incorporated. May I help you?"

There was silence on the other end of the phone. Then I heard light breathing. I put my hand over the receiver and whispered to Jessi, "I think it's a goof call."

"Say hello again," Jessi suggested.

"Hello? Hello?"

"Is this Mallory?" asked a familiar-sounding voice.

"Yes, it is. Who's this?"

"It's Kristy Thomas."

My heart practically stopped beating. "It's Kristy Thomas," I told Jessi. "You know, the president of the Baby-sitters Club." And then — I have no idea where these words came from, but I found myself speaking them — I said to Kristy, "Need a baby-sitter?"

Jessi giggled.

"No, I do not need a baby-sitter," Kristy replied hotly.

"Well, then. How may I help you?"

"You may tell me if you're holding a meeting of something called Kids Incorporated right now," said Kristy.

"Yes, we are."

"And you hold your meetings every Monday, Wednesday, and Friday afternoon from five-thirty until six?"

"We plan to."

"Copy-cats."

That made me pause. Jessi and I *were* being copy-cats. But then I remembered the awful meetings of the Baby-sitters Club that I'd attended.

"Well, you guys wouldn't let me join *your* club," I pointed out.

"We *tried* to let you," said Kristy. "But we have to be very careful about who joins. We need experienced, reliable sitters. You can't take chances where little kids are concerned."

"But I *am* experienced and reliable," I said.

"You didn't pass the test."

"That test was unfair. Even a doctor couldn't have passed it."

I heard Kristy sigh. Then she said, "I don't think your club is going to work. There aren't enough of you. You don't have any experience. You'll never get jobs."

"For your information, we've already gotten two," I told her.

"You have?"

"Yes. Now, if you don't have anything else to say, I'm going to get off the phone so some more calls can come in."

"Fine," said Kristy. "Good-bye."

"Good-bye." I nearly slammed the receiver

down, but I stopped myself in time. That would have been too rude. Even for Kristy Thomas.

"What was that all about?" Jessi wanted to know.

I told her.

"You know something?" said Jessi. "I have a funny feeling we haven't heard the last of the Baby-sitters Club."

CHAPTER 12

"Hey, Squirt! Hey, Squirt! Over here! Oh, what a good boy!"

Squirt Ramsey had just taken his first tentative steps all by himself, and Jessi and Becca and I were there to see him. Our sitting job at the Ramseys' was on a sunny Wednesday afternoon, and the four of us were out in the front yard. Squirt was the center of attention and loving it. He grinned, then blew a raspberry at Becca.

"Okay, Squirt. Stand up. Try again!" said Becca encouragingly. She pulled Squirt to his feet, waited until he was standing steadily, then let go of him.

"Come here! You can do it!" Jessi called, her arms outstretched.

"Walk to Jessi, Squirt," Becca added.

Step, step, step, step, step, step. Squirt's baby shoes plodded through the grass until — thump — he landed on his bottom.

"Six steps! Six steps, Jessi!" cried Becca. "That's Squirt's new record!"

This time I pulled Squirt to his feet. "Okay, let 'er rip," I said, and Squirt headed for Becca. But he only took four steps before he fell. He went down on his hands and knees. We all expected him to cry, but he came up laughing.

Becca began to giggle. "You are so goofy, Squirt," she said.

"Becca, maybe Squirt's getting tired of walking," Jessi suggested.

"Could I push him around in his stroller?" asked Becca. "I'd stay on the sidewalk and the driveway. I wouldn't go on the grass."

"Sure," replied Jessi. "That's fine. I'll go get the stroller for you."

Jessi disappeared into the garage and returned a few moments later with Squirt's stroller. "Here you go," she said to Becca.

"Thanks!" Becca heaved Squirt awkwardly into the stroller and began walking him proudly down the driveway.

"Becca is awfully good with him," I pointed out, as Jessi and I watched them from the front steps.

"It's a recent thing," Jessi replied. "Just since we moved here. I think it's because she's at home so much. In Oakley she was always off with Sandy or Kara or Raun or someone. But

she doesn't have any friends here in Stoneybrook."

I nodded thoughtfully. "How are things
going for you?" I asked. "I mean in ballet class
and at school?"

"It's funny. In my ballet class I'm the only
black kid, but almost everyone has been really
nice to me. Oh, there are a couple of girls who
don't speak to me, but, well, mostly the teach-
ers and students are so wrapped up in dancing
that they don't notice what color you are. I
mean, this is a *serious* school."

I smiled.

"But at *our* school?" Jessi went on. "Where
there are some other black kids?"

"Yeah?"

"Things are better, I guess, but not great."

"At least they *are* better, though," I said
positively.

"That's true. It's been days since Benny Ott
shot a rubber band at me."

"Well, that's something. Boy, I'd sure like
to shoot *him* sometime. Don't you wish we
were back in second grade so we could just
give him cooties and that would be the end of
it?"

"Yeah," said Jessi, laughing. "Hey, Becca!
Not too close to the street, okay? Bring Squirt
back here, or stick to the sidewalk," she called.

"Okay," Becca called back.

"Boy, does she need friends," Jessi said quietly.

"Yeah. I can't believe no one will play with her."

"Mama could use some friends, too. It would be nice to meet the neighbors."

I nodded. And suddenly I remembered another sunny day about a year ago. It was a Saturday and a new baby-sitter was taking care of Claire, Nicky, Byron, and me. Her name was Stacey McGill, and she and her parents had moved to Stoneybrook just a month or two earlier. The five of us were sitting at the kitchen table eating a snack and, because I'd never moved, I'd asked Stacey how moving from New York to Stoneybrook had felt.

"Well," Stacey had replied, "it wasn't easy. I didn't want to leave New York, but everyone here has been so *nice* to us."

I remembered Stacey describing how people had come by with casseroles and cookies, with flowers and homemade fudge, with directions to the train station, beauty parlor, malls, and movie theaters, and even with tips on which was the best grocery store. "A lady from something called the Welcome Wagon came by," she'd added. "She handed us coupons for special deals at restaurants, a listing of the

105

doctors and dentists in Stoneybrook, some samples from this gourmet food store, and a lot of other Stoneybrook stuff."

I looked at the Ramseys' empty yard and empty front porch (except for Jessi and me). I knew no neighbors had come by with gifts or helpful information. How mean.

"I have a feeling this is a silly question," I said, "but has a lady from the Welcome Wagon dropped by?"

"Are you kidding?" replied Jessi.

"I didn't think she had."

"Why did you want to know?"

"Oh, I was just remembering something," I told her.

"What?"

"It isn't important."

Becca had gotten tired of pushing Squirt around and had wheeled him back to Jessi and me. "Can I play with my bubble-maker?" she asked.

"Sure, that's a great idea," Jessi answered. "Go on inside and get it. Do you remember how to mix the bubble solution?"

"Yup!" replied Becca and ran through the front door.

"You should see this toy she's got," said Jessi. "It's amazing. It makes bubbles that are almost as big as she is."

"Are you serious?"

"One hundred per cent."

Becca returned carrying a wand with a loop of flat rope attached to it, and a mixing bowl full of sudsy water. She set the bowl on the front lawn, held onto the wand, dipped the rope into the solution, then opened it into a circle as she swung her arm slowly around. An enormous bubble formed through the rope. Becca expertly closed it off and it floated away.

"Look at that! Look at that one!" she cried. "It's my biggest ever!"

"Becca says that about every bubble," Jessi whispered to me.

But the bubble really *was* huge. It wasn't quite as big as Becca, but it was certainly bigger than Squirt. He could easily have fit inside it.

Becca made another bubble, and another.

At the house across the street, the door opened and a face looked out.

Becca made a fourth bubble.

A little girl stepped onto the porch.

Becca made a fifth bubble.

The girl tiptoed down her front stoop and halfway across the lawn to watch Becca and her bubbles.

"Look," I said, nudging Jessi.

"I know," she whispered.

The girl reached the street, crossed it care-

fully, and ran to Becca. "How do you do that?"
she asked "Those are the biggest —"

"Amy!" called a sharp voice. An angry-
looking woman was standing on the porch
across the street.

Amy turned around. "Mom?"

"Come here this instant," said her mother
stiffly. Then she went back in the house,
slamming the door behind her.

Amy reluctantly left Becca and her bubbles
and crossed the street again.

"You see what I mean?" said Jessi bitterly.

But I didn't answer her. I had just seen
something else. Another little face was peeking
at us, this time through a hedge at the side of
the Ramseys' house. I recognized the face.

"Charlotte?" I called.

Charlotte Johanssen pushed her way between two bushes in the hedge and stood
timidly at the side of the yard, her hands
behind her back. I knew Charlotte slightly. She
was eight years old and lived nearby. The girls
in the Baby-sitters Club sat for her, but Stacey
McGill had been Charlotte's favorite sitter.

"Hi, Charlotte!" I said. "Come on over. You
want to meet some new people?"

Charlotte didn't answer.

"She's shy," I whispered to Jessi. I turned

back to Charlotte. "Did you want to see what was happening at Stacey's old house?"

Charlotte shook her head. "My mom told me to come over," she said. At last she stepped toward us. When she reached us, she went on quietly, "Mom said there was a girl here just my age who could be my new friend."

"She *did?*" said Jessi incredulously.

Charlotte nodded. Then she looked at Becca, who was concentrating on making her bubbles. "Is that her? Is she eight years old?"

"She sure is," replied Jessi. "Her name's Becca. I bet she could teach you how to make big bubbles, too."

"Really?"

"Of course. Hey, Becca!" Jessi called. "Come here. Someone wants to play with you."

Becca turned around. Her eyes widened when she saw Charlotte. "Hi!" she called. She ran over to us.

"Hi," said Charlotte, a little smile creeping onto her lips. "That's neat, that bubble thing. Can you really show me how to use it?"

" 'Course!" cried Becca. "Come here. Come stand out in the middle of the yard."

"Okay," replied Charlotte. "Oh, I almost forgot." She took her hands from behind her back and held out a foil-wrapped package.

"This is for you," she said to Jessi. "I mean, for your whole family. It's banana bread from my mom and dad. Oh, and my mom wants your family to come over for supper next Saturday, but she's going to call your mom tonight so they can talk about the details."

"Hey, thanks!" said Jessi. "That's really nice."

Charlotte joined Becca with the bubble-maker, and I pulled Squirt into my lap. Jessi looked down at the banana bread and then up at me.

"Maybe," she said, "it won't be so bad here after all."

"Yeah," I agreed. "Some things just take time."

CHAPTER 13

Okay, you guys. How are we going to solve our problem? (At least we all agree that there is a problem.) You know, in a way, this is a nice problem to have — being too busy. In the past when we've written about club problems in our notebook they were pretty bad ones, like we were all mad and not speaking to each other, or there was a member among us who seemed about ready to defect. At least this problem just means that we're really successful. Still, we have to do something about it....

When I read Mary Anne's notebook entry a few weeks later, I almost laughed. The answer was so obvious. Ask *me* to join the club! But they had blown that with their stupid digestive-system test. And then they had gotten themselves in hot water. It wouldn't be much longer, though, until they saw what they had to do. In fact, by the end of the meeting they were holding the day Mary Anne wrote about the problem, they were on their way to solving things.

The meeting started off on the wrong foot because Kristy and Dawn were in bad moods and Claudia couldn't find this package of Ring-Dings she'd hidden in her room.

"Did one of you guys take it?" asked Claudia accusingly.

"Are you kidding? That trash?" replied Dawn. "I wouldn't touch it with a ten-foot pole. You know, you're going to rot your teeth, Claudia. Your face is going to break out and people will call you — "

"They will call me *happy*," Claudia interrupted her, "because that's what I am when I eat Ring-Dings. So you can just stop lecturing me about food. If I ate health food, I'd probably turn into a rabbit like you. A skinny, pale rabbit. I'd — "

"Shut up," said Kristy. "You two are wasting our time. This meeting started five minutes ago and all we've done is crab at each other and go on a Ring-Ding hunt. But believe me, we've got a problem. Mary Anne, open up our notebook."

"Yes, *sir*," said Mary Anne sarcastically. She'd come to the meeting in a good mood, but by now even she was feeling cross.

Kristy held up the club's appointment book, which was opened to the calendar pages. "See this?" she barked.

"Yeah," said Dawn, who was not happy about having been called a skinny, pale rabbit. "So?"

"It is all full," said Kristy flatly. "For two weeks."

"Correct me if I'm wrong, but I thought that was the point of this club," said Claudia. "To sign up jobs. And when we do that, we fill up the calendar."

"Save the sarcasm," Kristy told her. "Of course that was the point. But what happens if someone calls needing a sitter during the next two weeks?"

"We ask Logan or Shannon to take the job," said Mary Anne. "That's what they're there for. They're our back-ups." (Logan Bruno and Shannon Kilbourne are two associate club

113

members, which means that they don't come to meetings, but they're called on to take jobs no one else can take.)

"I guess so," said Kristy. "I mean, I know so. It just seems to me that they shouldn't be quite this necessary to us. . . . Boy, do we need Stacey back."

"Yeah . . ." the others said and fell silent. They all missed Stacey, especially Claudia, who had been her best friend.

The phone rang then. Kristy, perched in the director's chair, adjusted her visor and reached for the receiver. "Keep your fingers crossed that this is a call for at least a year from now."

That brought a smile to Claudia's face, anyway. The girls listened to Kristy's end of the conversation. "Hi, Mrs. Prezzioso. . . . Oh, fine, thanks. How's Jenny? . . . Good. . . . Thursday afternoon? I'll get back to you right away. . . . Okay. . . . Sure. Good-bye."

Kristy hung up the phone. "Somebody around here wasn't crossing her fingers," she said. "Mrs. Prezzioso needs someone for this Thursday afternoon."

Mary Anne closed the notebook she'd been writing in and took the record book from Kristy. "Let me handle this," she said. "It's my job." She looked at the appointment calendar. "What's

114

the big deal, Kristy? You and Claudia are both free that afternoon.''

"Claudia and I are both sitting that *evening*. You know our parents won't let us take two jobs on the same day, at least not during the week. We'd never get our homework done."

"Well, I'll call Logan," said Mary Anne happily. She didn't look the least bit upset. That was because Logan Bruno is Mary Anne's boyfriend, and she loves any chance to call him.

Mary Anne knew Logan's number by heart. She dialed it, then pulled the phone into a corner and turned her back on the other club members. "Hello, Logan?" they could hear her say. "It's me. Yeah. . . . Mmphh, mmblmmbl." She dropped her voice so low that even though Kristy, Dawn, and Claudia leaned over as far as they dared, they couldn't hear what she was saying. And she didn't raise it again until the only thing left to say was, "Good-bye."

"Well?" asked Kristy.

"He's free," Mary Anne replied. "You can call Mrs. Prezzioso now."

As soon as Kristy had done so, *another* call came in for Thursday.

"Shannon Kilbourne is our only hope," said Kristy, who called her immediately. Luckily, Shannon was free, too.

"That was close," commented Claudia.

"I'll say," agreed Kristy. "Too close. We've *got* to do something. At this point, even a sitter who was only available in the afternoons would help us."

"We have to find another club member," said Dawn, "and that's that."

"You know," said Mary Anne, "when Stacey and I went to Sea City with the Pikes, Mallory was awfully helpful. She wasn't even supposed to be a baby-sitter, but she automatically watched her brothers and sisters all the time, especially in the water. She remembered to see that they were wearing sunblock, and we knew that if we had to split up into groups, like when we were playing miniature golf, we could put her in charge of one of the groups and not have a thing to worry about."

"You know when we held the playgroup last summer?" began Kristy.

"Yeah?" said Claudia.

"Well, Mallory did more than just help out. When she walked the kids from her neighborhood over to Stacey's house, she taught them about crossing the street. She didn't have to do that, she just did it."

"And," began Claudia, "when she and I baby-sat at the Perkinses' she didn't do anything really wrong. She was mostly clumsy,

116

like when she spilled the milk and broke the glass. She did make a mistake with the snack and with Chewy, but that wasn't so bad. . . ."

"I just remembered something," spoke up Dawn. "Mrs. Pike called my mom last night to tell her about some PTA thing, and they started talking about Nicky's hand. It turns out that it was a total accident. It happened so fast that *no* one could have prevented it." Dawn explained what had happened. "So it wasn't Mallory's fault at all — and we blamed her for it," she finished up.

"Oops," said Kristy.

Claudia cleared her throat nervously. "Um," she said, "I didn't want to admit this before, but I didn't know anything about the divestive system before we made up that test."

"It's di-*ges*-tive," Dawn told her, "and neither did I."

"Me neither," added Mary Anne. She and Dawn and Claudia looked at Kristy.

"Oh, all right, neither did I," said Kristy. "Well, not much."

"Did you know about tourniquets?" Claudia asked her.

"Only that you have to let a doctor remove them."

"You know, it took us hours to make up that test," said Mary Anne slowly, "and not because we had so many questions to choose from. It was because we had to look everything up."

Kristy hung her head. "I guess we were pretty unfair to Mallory."

"Yeah," agreed the others.

"But we do have to be careful," Kristy went on. "Little kids are important. I mean, everyone is important, but we have a responsibility to the kids we take care of, and to their parents. We can't sign up sitters who are going to let accidents happen or who wouldn't know what to do if a kid got sick."

"That's true," said Dawn, "but I don't think we should expect more from anyone else than we do from ourselves. And I think Mallory knows just as much about children as we do."

"You're right," said Kristy. She paused. Then she added, "Well, shall I call Mallory and ask her back?"

"Yes!" cried Claudia, Dawn, and Mary Anne.

When the phone rang in the hall outside my bedroom, Jessi and I hoped desperately that it was a job call. We hadn't had a single sitting job since that Wednesday afternoon at the Ramseys'. Needless to say, I was pretty disappointed to hear Kristy Thomas's voice on the other end of the line — that is, until I listened to what she had to say.

118

"Mallory, we were unfair," she began. "The test was unfair. We see that now. So the reason I'm calling is to find out if you want to try joining the club again as a junior sitter. You know, afternoons only. All you'll have to do is go on one baby-sitting job with another club member. I promise she won't make you nervous."

"You want me to join the Baby-sitters Club!" I cried. I glanced up and saw Jessi's face. She looked stricken. "What about Jessi Ramsey?" I asked Kristy. And then I heard myself say, "Either both of us join or neither of us does. You have to take all of Kids Incorporated."

Jessi smiled broadly.

I listened to the muffled sounds on the other end of the phone that meant Kristy had put her hand over the receiver and was discussing things with her friends. At long last she said, "Mallory? Can you and Jessi both come to the next meeting?"

"We'll be there," I said simply and hung up the phone. Then I looked at Jessi. "I think we made it!" I told her.

CHAPTER 14

Jessi and I were nervous wrecks waiting for the next meeting of the Baby-sitters Club. We spent the afternoon before that meeting together at my house.

"Are we crazy to be giving up Kids Incorporated?" I asked Jessi. We were sitting on the back porch, since Vanessa and two of her friends had taken over our bedroom.

"I don't know," replied Jessi with a sigh. "I mean, I haven't met the girls in the club, so I don't know what we're getting into. But we weren't having much luck with Kids Incorporated, were we?"

"No. Just two jobs — and all those meetings! But I hope . . ."

"Hope what?"

"That we can all get along."

"Well," said Jessi, "one thing I've learned since I moved here is that you can get along with people even if you're not good friends with them. You know, like I'm getting along in school okay, but you're my only real friend."

"That doesn't sound so good," I told her.

"No, no. What I mean is —"

"That's okay," I interrupted her. "I think I know what you mean. The girls in the club are older than we are, so maybe we won't end up close friends, but we can get along. We can work together. Besides, you and I have each other."

"Always," said Jessi firmly.

"Always," I repeated. I looked at Jessi and knew that we were best friends.

At 5:25 that afternoon, Jessi and I stood on Claudia Kishi's front stoop. I rang the bell.

My hand was shaking.

"Relax," said Jessi.

"I can't."

Claudia answered the door. "Hi, you guys," she said. "Come on upstairs."

Jessi and I followed Claudia through her living room, up the stairs, and along the hallway to her bedroom.

The other club members were waiting for us.

"Hi," said Kristy. She looked just as nervous as I felt.

"Hi," replied Jessi and I at the same time.

Claudia closed the door behind us.

Kristy, her visor safely on her head, got up from the director's chair and said, "You must be Jessi Ramsey. I'm Kristy Thomas. And here," she went on, pointing to Dawn and Mary Anne, who were sitting side by side on the bed, "are Dawn Schafer and Mary Anne Spier. That's Claudia Kishi, the one foraging for junk food."

Claudia grinned. She'd found a giant box of Cracker Jacks and she passed it around as Jessi and I settled ourselves on the floor.

"So you moved into Stacey's house," Mary Anne said to Jessi.

Jessi nodded.

"Right into her old room," I added.

"Where'd you move from?" Kristy wanted to know.

Jessi told them.

"Do you like Stoneybrook?" asked Dawn.

"I do. I'm glad we moved here."

"It's — I . . ." Jessi paused.

"Not everyone has been exactly friendly," I tried to explain.

"Oh," said Kristy suddenly, looking slightly embarrassed. "I see."

Thank goodness the phone rang then. Jessi and I watched the girls set up a job.

When they were done, Kristy said, "We

were lucky. Claudia happened to be free that afternoon. But there have been lots of days lately when none of us was free. That's why we need you two. If you could take some of the afternoon jobs for us, it would free us to sit in the evenings, and that would be a big help."

I frowned. "So are you asking us to join the club or not?" I said boldly.

"I wish I could say we are," replied Kristy, "but we can't. Not yet."

"But you said —"

"I said no more unfair tests. We do want to see you in action, though. Especially Jessi. We don't know her at all."

"She's great with kids!" I told the girls enthusiastically. "You should see her with her baby brother."

"We just have to make sure," said Kristy firmly. "All we want to do is send each of you on one sitting job with a club member. I promise we won't interfere. We'll just step back and watch — and let you be in charge. If things go okay, you're in the club. Sound fair?"

I looked at Jessi. We nodded. "It's fair," I told Kristy.

"But," spoke up Jessi, "I have to ask one thing."

"Money?" asked Kristy. "Club responsibilities?"

"No," said Jessi, looking down at her hands. "It's more complicated than that. And I better bring it up now before I join the club."

"Jess, what is it?" I asked worriedly. She hadn't told me about any problem.

"Well," began Jessi, sounding awfully serious. "The thing is, so far I've only baby-sat at Mal's house and mine. But a lot of families around here don't seem, um, they don't seem to like me. Because I'm black. So I'm wondering — what if your clients don't want me to sit for them? I mean, that's not going to help you at all. It might even hurt the club."

I watched Kristy and her friends exchange glances.

"We hadn't thought of that," said Mary Anne slowly. "We don't really know if it's going to be a problem."

"*We* don't care that you're black," added Claudia. "After all, I'm Japanese. Well, Japanese-American. No one minds that."

"But there really are problems," I said. I told the girls what had happened when Amy had wanted to play with Becca and her bubble-maker.

"Whoa," said Dawn under her breath.

"And that's not the only time something like

that has happened," Jessi went on. "Plus, there are other things. None of the neighbors has come by. Well, hardly any. Neither did the Welcome Wagon lady."

"But things are changing, or else beginning to happen very slowly," I pointed out. "The Johanssens invited the Ramseys over for dinner, and Charlotte and Becca are getting to be friends."

"Benny Ott stopped shooting rubber bands at me," added Jessi.

"Who's Benny Ott?" asked Kristy, smiling.

"This jerky boy in our grade," I replied. "He's always doing stuff like making faces behind the teacher's back or throwing spitballs. Once, he brought fake barf to school. And this girl, Danni, took one look at it and barfed for real."

The girls in the Baby-sitters Club laughed.

"Benny Ott sounds just like Alan Gray," said Kristy, giggling.

"Who's Alan Gray?" Jessi and I asked at the same time. (We had to stop the conversation long enough to hook pinkies and say "jinx.")

"Alan Gray," Kristy replied, "is the Benny Ott of the eighth grade."

"You mean boys are still weird in eighth grade?"

"Definitely," said Kristy.

"Sort of," said Dawn.

"It depends," said Claudia.

"Not really," said Mary Anne.

We started to laugh again. Then Claudia grew serious. "We're getting off the subject," she said. "What about Jessi's problem?"

There was a moment of silence. No one seemed to want to speak. At long last Kristy said, "You know what I think? I think we'll just have to face the problem if it happens. It's hard for me to imagine it happening, though. I mean, I can't see any of our regular customers — the Newtons, my mom and Watson, the Barretts, the Perkinses, the Rodowskys — I can't see any of them saying they don't want Jessi to sit. If it does happen with anyone, though, I'll tell you one thing — *I* wouldn't sit for them, either."

"Me neither," said Claudia, Mary Anne, and Dawn. (It took a moment for the three of them all to hook pinkies and say "jinx.")

"Really?" asked Jessi, awed.

"Really," replied Kristy. "We'll be like the Three Musketeers. One for all and all for one. Only we'll be the Six Musketeers."

Ring, ring.

Claudia grabbed for the phone and got it just before Kristy did. "Hello, Baby-sitters

Club," she said. "*Stacey?* STACE! I don't believe it! Hi! We haven't spoken in two whole
days! Guess what? We're having a club meeting. Everyone is sitting right here. . . . What?
. . . Oh." Claudia held her hand over the
receiver and whispered to us, "That's why she
called. Because she knew we'd all be here."
She uncovered the phone. "Listen to this,"
she said to Stacey. "We finally replaced you.
Or we're about to, anyway."

Jessi and I grinned at each other.

"With Mallory Pike and a friend of hers,
Jessi Ramsey," Claudia went on. "Yeah, the
family who moved into your house." Claudia
listened for a moment and then began to laugh.
She covered the receiver again. "Stacey just
said, 'You mean I was so good it took *two*
people to replace me?' "

Kristy giggled. "Let me talk to her," she
said.

For the next few minutes the phone was
passed around from person to person. Even
Jessi and I said hi to Stacey. At last Kristy grew
fidgety. "Okay, you guys," she said. "You
know the rule about personal calls during
meetings. It was great to talk to Stacey, but
we better hang up. Our clients might be trying
to reach us."

127

Claudia hung up reluctantly. Now that I had my own best friend, I had a pretty good idea just how much Claudia missed Stacey.

Anyway, it was a good thing they said good-bye, because as soon as Claudia hung up the phone, it started ringing again. And by the time the meeting was over, trial sitting jobs had been lined up for both Jessi and me. I would be sitting with Claudia for Jamie and Lucy Newton, and Jessi would be sitting with Dawn two days later for a little boy named Jackie Rodowsky.

"Bring a crash helmet along," Dawn told Jessi with a grin. "Jackie is the most accident-prone kid you'll ever meet."

"Oh, no!" cried Jessi. "I hope I'm ready for this."

But I knew that we were. Jessi and I could handle anything.

CHAPTER 15

"Hi-hi!" called Jamie Newton. "Hi, Claudia! Hi, Mallory. . . . How come Lucy and I get *two* sitters today?"

"Because you are very lucky," his mother told him. "Come on in, girls."

It was the day of my trial sitting job. Claudia and I had just arrived at the home of four-year-old Jamie Newton and his baby sister, Lucy. I was nervous, but not nearly as nervous as I'd been when I'd sat at the Perkinses'. For some reason, I just knew everything was going to be okay. The power of positive thinking, my mother would say.

Mrs. Newton showed me where everything was (even though Claudia knew already), and told us to take the kids outdoors since the weather was so beautiful.

"Lucy's stroller is by the back door. She loves to be pushed around in the yard. And Jamie will probably want to play on his swingset. Oh, by the way, the washing machine repairman is going to come over. I hope. He was supposed to show up sometime between nine and five today, and he hasn't arrived yet. All you have to do is point him in the direction of the washing machine. He knows what the problem is."

"Okay," said Claudia confidently.

Mrs. Newton waved good-bye to Jamie, who was running around with a towel pinned to his back, pretending he was Superman. Then she kissed Lucy on her nose. "I'll be back at five-thirty," she told Claudia and me. "Good luck, Mallory."

"Thanks," I replied.

"Okay," said Claudia, after Mrs. Newton had left. "You're on your own, Mallory. Just pretend I'm not here." Claudia sat down at the kitchen table and tried to look invisible.

I drew in a deep breath and let it out slowly. "Right," I said.

Lucy was sitting in her walker, scooting around the kitchen. I picked her up and put on the sweater and little sneakers Mrs. Newton had said she should wear outdoors. When she began to whimper, I said softly to her, "I know you don't know me, Lucy-Goose, but it's going to be okay. It's really going to be okay." I had learned how to talk soothingly like that when

Claire was born. She was fussy from her colic and always seemed to need attention. Lucy quieted down.

"Jamie?" I called.

"Yeah?" he replied. He bounded into the kitchen, towel flying. "I am Superman!" he roared. "I'm going to trample that old King Corn."

"King Corn?" I repeated.

"He means King Kong," Claudia whispered.

"Oh. . . . Hey!" I cried, looking out the window. "Jamie! I think King Kong is in the backyard!"

"Really?" said Jamie, but I could tell he knew I was kidding.

"Yeah. Put your sweater on. Let's go!"

It took a few minutes to get ready. First I settled Lucy in her stroller. Then I had to help Jamie repin his towel so that it was outside of his sweater. But at last we were in the bright sunshine and the crisp air. Claudia followed us to the back door, where she stayed, watching us through the screen.

Jamie made a beeline for his swingset, jumped onto a swing, pushed himself back, and began pumping his legs. "Hi-hi!" he called as he whizzed back and forth. "Hi-hi, Mallory!"

"Hi-hi, Superman," I replied.

I pushed Lucy around the yard. She babbled

to herself, tried to catch bugs that flew by, and sometimes just sat quietly, gazing up at the blue, blue sky.

This wasn't so bad. In fact it was easy.

Just a few moments after I'd been thinking how easy the job was, I heard the Newtons' phone ring.

"I'll get it!" Claudia called from the back door. "Don't worry about it, Mallory." (I'd almost forgotten she was there.)

I listened to Claudia's feet clatter upstairs to the Newton's kitchen. The next thing I knew she was yelling out the window to me, "Mallory! Hey, Mal! I'm really sorry but I have to go home for a few minutes. Mimi's in some kind of jam. I'll be back as soon as I can!"

(Mimi, Claudia's grandmother, had a stroke last summer and can't use her right hand anymore. She has trouble speaking, too. I hoped the problem wasn't serious.)

"Okay!" I called to Claudia. "No problem. We'll stay right here. We'll be fine!"

So we did and we were. I mean, we were eventually — but things got kind of hectic for awhile. First, Myriah and Gabbie Perkins came over. That wasn't the hectic part. It was fine.

The girls knocked at the Newtons' back gate. "Jamie?" I could hear Myriah call. "Are you there? Hi-hi! It's Gabbie and me, Myriah!"

"Mallory!" Jamie called from the swing. "My friends are here. Can I let them in?"

"Sure," I replied, even though neither Mrs. Newton nor Claudia had said anything one way or the other about having friends over.

Jamie unlatched the gate and Myriah and Gabbie entered the yard. Myriah was wearing a T-shirt that said I'M THE BIG SISTER. Gabbie was wearing one that said I'M THE MIDDLE SISTER.

"Do you like our shirts?" asked Myriah. "Laura Beth has one that says 'I'm the little sister.' "

"It's teeny-tiny," added Gabbie.

"How is your sister?" I asked. "Are you glad to have her home from the hospital?"

"Oh, definitely," said Myriah, sounding very grown-up.

"Yes, definitely," added Gabbie. "Sometimes Mommy lets us hold her."

"That's terrific," I told them.

Myriah and Gabbie had just joined Jamie on the swingset when I heard something pull up in the Newtons' driveway. Not Mrs. Newton, I thought, checking my watch. I ran to the gate, opened it a crack, and peeped out. A truck was parked there. On its side were the words ACE REPAIR COMPANY. The washing machine repairman! I'd forgotten all about him

— and I didn't even know where the washer was.

I didn't lose my cool, though. I decided that Jamie, Gabbie, and Myriah were okay by themselves in the yard for a few minutes. Then I lifted Lucy out of her stroller and joined the repairman.

"Hi," I said.

"Hi, there," he replied, reaching into the back of his truck for some tools. "You got a broken washer? A leaky one?"

"Yup. Come on inside." I figured that a washing machine could only be in a laundry room or a basement, and I knew the Newtons didn't have a laundry room, so I showed the man to the cellar.

I had just turned on the light for him when the phone rang. Still holding Lucy, I dashed upstairs to answer it. As the voice on the other end was telling me she'd dialed a wrong number, I looked out the kitchen window into the backyard — just in time to see Jamie tumble off one of the swings.

" 'Bye!" I said hurriedly to the woman on the phone. "Okay, Lucy-Goose. Hang on. We're going for a ride!"

I tore outside and ran to Jamie, who was crying loudly. When I reached him, I set Lucy carefully on the grass.

"Where do you hurt?" I asked Jamie.

"My kneeeee!" he wailed, pointing to his right knee.

I rolled up the leg of his jeans. "Surprise!" I said. "What do you know, Jamie? No scrape. Just a bump, I guess." (His knee looked fine.)

Myriah and Gabbie crowded in for a look at the wound. The three of them began comparing stories about injuries. Jamie stopped crying.

I rocked back on my heels and started toward Lucy, who was sitting happily in the grass.

"Good job," said a voice behind me.

I jumped.

"Sorry," said Claudia. "I didn't mean to scare you, but I got back here just in time to see how you handled all this. You did fine. I guess you showed the repairman where the machine is?"

"Sure, no problem," I said casually, but I was shaking inside. Thank goodness she thought everything had gone well. "Jamie's — Jamie's fall was an accident," I added quickly. "I mean, I *had* to go inside with the Ace repairman and —"

"Don't worry about it," said Claudia. "Accidents do happen. We all know that. Even the best baby-sitter can't prevent every accident."

I let out a sigh of relief.

"Well," said Claudia, "we'll have to make a

club decision, of course, but I don't think there's any doubt about it — you'll be joining the Baby-sitters Club."

"Oh! Oh, really? I mean, thank you! Thanks a lot! That's great!"

"Goo-goo," agreed Lucy.

Claudia and I laughed.

I thought about Jessi. I was positive she would become a club member, too.

Club member. That sounded fantastic. I, Mallory Pike, was going to become a junior member of the Baby-sitters Club! So was Jessi.

We had made it.

Dear Reader,

In *Hello, Mallory*, Mallory Pike, formerly a sitting charge of the Baby-sitters Club, finally becomes a full-fledged member herself. In earlier books, Mallory had expressed frustration at having a baby-sitter when she felt she was a perfectly capable baby-sitter herself. Also, I had received a number of letters from readers asking for a younger member of the BSC, since many readers were Mallory's age or younger. Then I decided that Mallory needed a best friend, so I created one for her — Jessi Ramsey.

Although I usually compare myself to Mary Anne, I am like Mallory Pike in several ways. I am the oldest in my family (even though I have only one younger sister and no brothers). I was just as horse-crazy as Mallory is. And I enjoyed writing and illustrating stories. Like Mallory, I also had a mouthful of braces, which I hated!

Happy reading,

Ann M. Martin

L. GODWIN

Ann M. Martin

About the Author

ANN MATTHEWS MARTIN was born on August 12, 1955. She grew up in Princeton, NJ, with her parents and her younger sister, Jane.

Although Ann used to be a teacher and then an editor of children's books, she's now a full-time writer. She gets the ideas for her books from many different places. Some are based on personal experiences. Others are based on childhood memories and feelings. Many are written about contemporary problems or events.

All of Ann's characters, even the members of the Baby-sitters Club, are made up. (So is Stoneybrook.) But many of her characters are based on real people. Sometimes Ann names her characters after people she knows, other times she chooses names she likes.

In addition to the Baby-sitters Club books, Ann Martin has written many other books for children. Her favorite is *Ten Kids, No Pets* because she loves big families and she loves animals. Her favorite Baby-sitters Club book is *Kristy's Big Day*. (By the way, Kristy is her favorite baby-sitter!)

Ann M. Martin now lives in New York with her cats, Gussie and Woody. Her hobbies are reading, sewing, and needlework — especially making clothes for children.

Notebook Pages

This Baby-sitters Club book belongs to _____.

I am _____ years old and in the _____

grade.

The name of my school is _____.

I got this BSC book from _____.

I started reading it on _____ and

finished reading it on _____.

The place where I read most of this book is _____.

My favorite part was when _____.

If I could change anything in the story, it might be the part when

_____.

My favorite character in the Baby-sitters Club is _____.

The BSC member I am most like is _____

because _____.

If I could write a Baby-sitters Club book it would be about ____

_____.

#14 Hello, Mallory

Mallory is very nervous about joining the Baby-sitters Club, especially after the BSC members start testing her. One group I'd be very nervous about joining is _____ .

One person who makes me really, really nervous is _____ .

When I'm nervous, I _____ .

In order to become a member of the Baby-sitters Club, Mallory has to prove herself worthy of membership. One time I had to show people I was good enough was when I _____ _____ . I showed them I was good enough by _____ .

If I were testing someone to make sure she or he was a good baby-sitter, I would make sure she or he _____ .

One thing a good baby-sitter always does is _____ .

One thing a baby-sitter should never, ever do is _____ .

If I were to start a Baby-sitters Club, I think these people would be the most qualified members: _____ , _____ , and _____ .

MALLORY'S

Age 2 —
Already
a fan of
reading

Age 10 —
Still a fan.
Waiting to
meet my
favorite
author.

SCRAPBOOK

Two of my favorite things—babysitting and Ben.

My family—all ten of us!

Read all the books
about **Mallory**
in the Baby-sitters Club series
by Ann M. Martin

THE BABY-SITTERS CLUB®

by Ann M. Martin

More titles... ▶

❑ MG47011-6 **#73 Mary Anne and Miss Priss**   **$3.50**
❑ MG47012-4 **#74 Kristy and the Copycat**   **$3.50**
❑ MG47013-2 **#75 Jessi's Horrible Prank**   **$3.50**
❑ MG47014-0 **#76 Stacey's Lie**   **$3.50**
❑ MG48221-1 **#77 Dawn and Whitney, Friends Forever**   **$3.50**
❑ MG48222-X **#78 Claudia and Crazy Peaches**   **$3.50**
❑ MG48223-8 **#79 Mary Anne Breaks the Rules**   **$3.50**
❑ MG48224-6 **#80 Mallory Pike, #1 Fan**   **$3.50**
❑ MG48225-4 **#81 Kristy and Mr. Mom**   **$3.50**
❑ MG48226-2 **#82 Jessi and the Troublemaker**   **$3.50**
❑ MG48235-1 **#83 Stacey vs. the BSC**   **$3.50**
❑ MG48228-9 **#84 Dawn and the School Spirit War**   **$3.50**
❑ MG48236-X **#85 Claudi Kishi, Live from WSTO**   **$3.50**
❑ MG48227-0 **#86 Mary Anne and Camp BSC**   **$3.50**
❑ MG48237-8 **#87 Stacey and the Bad Girls**   **$3.50**
❑ MG22872-2 **#88 Farewell, Dawn**   **$3.50**
❑ MG22873-0 **#89 Kristy and the Dirty Diapers**   **$3.50**
❑ MG45575-3 **Logan's Story Special Edition Readers' Request**   **$3.25**
❑ MG47118-X **Logan Bruno, Boy Baby-sitter**
                Special Edition Readers' Request   **$3.50**
❑ MG47756-0 **Shannon's Story Special Edition**   **$3.50**
❑ MG44240-6 **Baby-sitters on Board! Super Special #1**   **$3.95**
❑ MG44239-2 **Baby-sitters' Summer Vacation Super Special #2**   **$3.95**
❑ MG43973-1 **Baby-sitters' Winter Vacation Super Special #3**   **$3.95**
❑ MG42493-9 **Baby-sitters' Island Adventure Super Special #4**   **$3.95**
❑ MG43575-2 **California Girls! Super Special #5**   **$3.95**
❑ MG43576-0 **New York, New York! Super Special #6**   **$3.95**
❑ MG44963-X **Snowbound Super Special #7**   **$3.95**
❑ MG44962-X **Baby-sitters at Shadow Lake Super Special #8**   **$3.95**
❑ MG45661-X **Starring the Baby-sitters Club Super Special #9**   **$3.95**
❑ MG45674-1 **Sea City, Here We Come! Super Special #10**   **$3.95**
❑ MG47015-9 **The Baby-sitter's Remember Super Special #11**   **$3.95**
❑ MG48308-0 **Here Come the Bridesmaids Super Special #12**   **$3.95**

Available wherever you buy books...or use this order form.

Scholastic Inc., P.O. Box 7502, 2931 E. McCarty Street, Jefferson City, MO 65102

Please send me the books I have checked above. I am enclosing $ _____
(please add $2.00 to cover shipping and handling). Send check or money order—no
cash or C.O.D.s please.

Name _____ Birthdate _____

Address _____

City _____ State/Zip _____

THE BABY-SITTERS CLUB®

ALL NEW!

by Ann M. Martin

Meet the best friends you'll ever have!

Have you heard? The BSC has a new look—and more great stuff than ever before. An all-new scrapbook for each book's narrator! A letter from Ann M. Martin! Fill-in pages to personalize your copy! Order today!

❏ BBD22473-5	#1 **Kristy's Great Idea**	$3.50
❏ BBD22763-7	#2 **Claudia and the Phantom Phone Calls**	$3.50
❏ BBD25158-9	#3 **The Truth About Stacey**	$3.50
❏ BBD25159-7	#4 **Mary Anne Saves the Day**	$3.50
❏ BBD25160-0	#5 **Dawn and the Impossible Three**	$3.50

Available wherever you buy books, or use this order form.

Now THE BABY-SITTERS CLUB®

is a Video Club too!